BIRTHCAGE

BIRTHCAGE

This powerful collection of introspective stories explores the dynamics of conditioning, confinement, and the transformative journey of rebirth, offering a profound reflection on the paths to personal freedom and renewal.

BORISLAVA

www.birthcage.com | www.borislava.com

Library of Congress Control Number: 2024917647

Published in the United States by BIRTHCAGE ®

Front cover photo: Emmanuel Novelo

Back cover photo: Farid Novelo

Cover and Interior Design: Borislava Ratcheva

Cover photograph © 2020 by Borislava Ratcheva

ISBN: 979-8-9914000-0-8

English Ebook ISBN: 979-8-9914000-1-5

English Hardcover book with the complete work, including stories and images
ISBN: 979-8-9914000-7-7

Spanish Paperback ISBN: 979-8-9914000-3-9

Spanish Ebook ISBN: 979-8-9914000-4-6

Spanish Hardcover book with the complete work, including stories and images
ISBN: 979-8-9914000-2-2

First edition, October 2024

*To my higher self and angels that never
let me give up on my journey.*

Thank you! Love you!

CONTENTS

PREFACE

Years ago, I dreamed I was a photographer on a train. It was an old brown, rusted train like the ones from the 1950s with many wagons.

I was all the way at the back and wanted to get to the front, but first, I would have to pass through all the wagons.

As I moved through the train, I took pictures of the scenery outside from every window of every wagon. There were no other passengers on board, no one to bother me with my activity. The train was still moving and the scenery outside was changing quickly. At first, there were big green valleys and tall blue mountains. As I walked forward, it became more like the Savanna. And later, the blue mountains reappeared, but this time they were a little closer.

By the time I reached the front wagon, the outside scenery had changed, and now the train was passing through an urban area with many streets and buildings. There, I found the locomotive driver. To my surprise, the driver was a rough-looking guy with a menacing presence and sharp, calculating eyes. I told him to stop the train, but he refused. I worried that he might crash us somewhere in this dense urban area if I didn't do something to stop the train myself.

I had to act fast. I pushed him over and reached for the red hand break. Yanking it hard towards me, the train stopped at the last minute. The driver looked upset but didn't want to fight. I told him this was my train, and he needed to get off of it because, from now on, I would be the driver. To my surprise, he obeyed.

By that time, the landscape had changed again. It was a peaceful sunny day, and I was surrounded by many trees, rivers, and mountains. It felt like heaven had come to earth, and I couldn't help but get off the train myself to have a look around. I began walking through this magical land and enjoying its magnificence. After a while, I turned around to look back at the train. It seemed so out of place in this ecstatic landscape. I glanced at the back of the train and noticed it was surrounded by child playgrounds.

Then I woke up.

In bed, I thought about how the dream seemed to represent all I had been through. The photos I was taking were like the different things I had experienced in the various stages of my life. Now that I was in control of my train, I was responsible for showing the pictures and telling the world the stories. *Maybe they will help or inspire someone,* I thought.

PART ONE

ABANDONED

When I was seven months old, my parents left me in a weekly baby kindergarten. *You are probably thinking, what is a weekly baby kindergarten?* Strange things existed in communist Bulgaria back then. Imagine leaving your baby all week to an institution so parents could have more time to focus on more important things, like their careers. In the weekly kindergarten, you would drop off your baby on Monday morning and pick it up on Friday evening.

How convenient is that?

Why even have a child if you don't have the time and the energy to care for it?

I still don't understand.

To this day, I have memories of being left behind. The kindergarten felt like a little concentration camp or a prison. It was dark, and my cradle was propped beside a white brick wall. I can remember the cold and the feeling of being all alone. I remember crying and crying and crying.

One time, I cried so hard that instead of being yelled at, someone actually came, picked me up, and held me in her arms. I wanted to look out the window, but it was always too high. At the time, because

I was trying to reach with my tiny hands, she lifted me higher and nearer to the glass. I hoped to see my mother on the other side, but all I could see was the concrete sidewalk and a grass lawn. I guess we were in a basement. I can still feel the sadness and disappointment of that moment. All I wanted was for my mom to take me home, to be with me, to love me, and to hug me. *But she wasn't there.*

Growing up, I finally asked my mother why they left me alone at that weekly kindergarten.

She said: "Well, it was during the winter, and I was afraid you might get sick with pneumonia."

I knew they left me there before the winter, not because they feared I would get sick, but because she wanted to return to work. She wanted to make more money than the ninety percent of the total salary they offered for the first two years of maternity leave. She tried to build her career as a school principal.

Now, you might be thinking, maybe my parents were working far away, but the kindergarten they left me at was ten minutes walking distance from our apartment, three minutes from my mother's job, and five minutes from my father's job. It was precisely along my mother's way to work. Every day, instead of picking me up after work, she would walk past the building where she had left me and go home to relax without being bothered by the lonely baby she and my father had brought into this world.

For two years, I was left behind in this way, and after that, they sent me to the next childcare institution: kindergarten for kids between the ages of three and five.

BEATEN

From ages three to five, I was sent to the kindergarten for kids. I wouldn't say I liked it, but I had no choice. My grandparents were old, and no one else could care for me. The kindergarten was next to the school where my mother worked, but sometimes, they still forgot to pick me up. I had to stay and wait for them, feeling lonely and unwanted. The caretakers hated it, too, because one would have to stay with me until someone remembered I existed.

Life at the kindergarten was not fun. We ate the same food most of the week and were forced to finish it no matter what. After lunch, the caretakers forced us to sleep. Mandatory afternoon naps were from 2 pm to 4 pm. I was a very active child and often couldn't fall asleep.

One day, the teacher came in to check on us and noticed that I was lying there staring at the cute pear sticker on the board of my bed. I don't remember where I got that sticker from or how I was allowed to have it on my bed, but I loved getting lost in the patterns and colors. The pear was yellow with tiny brown spots and a tingle of red in the middle.

"Why are you not sleeping?" the caretaker asked me.

"I can't," I answered.

She then told me I must sleep, and I repeated that I could not fall asleep. I said this shouldn't be a problem because I was quiet and did not disturb anyone.

"I'm just looking at my sticker," I said.

Then she became angry because not only was I not asleep, but I had the guts to assert my right not to sleep. Her face turned bright red. She yanked out the little blanket I was cuddled in and started to beat me. She hit me all over and hissed at me that I must behave and obey anything she said. I felt lucky that at least she only used her hands. When someone uses their hands rather than an object, it hurts them too, and they stop sooner.

Later, at home, I told my parents what happened to me. I hoped that they would talk to the woman or do something. Instead, they told me she had been right and that I must sleep in the afternoons.

"But why did she beat me just because I couldn't fall asleep?" I said. "It wasn't my fault. I wasn't talking or doing anything wrong. I was lying in bed looking at my pear sticker."

They told me I needed to listen and follow everything I was instructed to do. I was upset. I couldn't understand how to force myself into sleep. *Was it even possible? Why didn't my parents understand me? Why were they never on my side?*

After that day, I learned to pretend. Every afternoon for two hours, I would lay in my bed with closed eyes, thinking about how much I hated all of this and wondering when it would end.

I promised myself that when I grew up, I would never tolerate physical abuse from anyone.

MOLESTED

During summer break, the kindergarten was closed for two months. The weather was nice, and I loved playing outside. My parents were busy. They didn't want to play or spend time with me, but one of our neighbors did. His name was Mr. Savchev. He was a fifty-something-year-old man living in a summer bungalow next to our small apartment building. He paid a lot of attention to me, and he befriended me. Almost every day, we played in the yard of his house.

One day, Mr. Savchev wanted to show me a new game. He called this game "pishinka" which is a made-up word that suggests the Bulgarian word "pishka", meaning peeing and also penis. The way he changed the word made it sound very innocent and quaint.

He started the game while seated on the bench outside his house with his legs spread wide. Then he unzipped his pants and took out his penis. I was watching from a distance and was surprised by its size. After all, I was only three or four years old. He encouraged me to come closer. I was so little that my head was precisely at the level of his crouch. I had learned that there were two genders and that he was of the opposite one, but until that moment, I had never seen grown-up male private parts.

Mr. Savchev told me it would be fun to open my mouth and put that thing in it. I was close to it now, and I thought there was no way I would put that massive thing into my small mouth. I thought it was gross and impossible, so I said, 'No.'

When he insisted, I grew agitated. I said: "No, no, no!"

Then he said it would be a good idea to go into the little tent he kept in his yard. I thought that was probably okay, and so I followed him. In the tent, there was a small inflatable mattress. He suggested I lay on it, so I did. I liked the softness of it. He told me to put my hands between my thighs, touch my crotch, and move my pelvis back and forward. I did this, and it felt good. Under his instructions (and, I suppose, my instincts), I had an orgasm.

It felt amazing, and I finally felt like I'd found some outlet, pleasure, and happiness in this life. While he watched me, he was holding his penis and moving his hand up and down. I don't remember if he ejaculated or not, but he looked pleased. In the end, he said this game was our secret, and I shouldn't tell anyone. I promised I wouldn't. He said that we could play again soon, and I agreed.

A few weeks later, another neighbor, a woman this time, was playing with me at her house. She asked me what kind of games I played with Mr. Savchev. I told her it was a secret, but since I really liked and trusted her, I whispered the name in her ear. She said she didn't know any game with that name and asked me to explain.

After I told her, she said it was probably not a good idea for me to continue playing with Mr. Savchev anymore.

"But why?" I asked. "It was pleasant."

She didn't answer. A few hours later, I was playing outside. My mother approached me and told me to go home right away.

There, with a very serious tone, she forbade me ever to play or talk with Mr. Savchev again. She said I shouldn't even say 'hi' to him anymore. I felt terrible. They made me feel like I had done something awful, but I obeyed and never played or spoke with him again.

Later, when I was grown up enough to understand what had happened, I wondered why they hadn't reported him. Was it because they didn't want to get into trouble, or were they afraid and tried to keep it a secret?

We never discussed it again, and I pretended it had never happened.

HUMILIATED

One night, while my mother and I were in the kitchen, she asked me where I was in the afternoon.

I was about five or six years old at the time. I knew my mother would get mad that I was playing in the house of one of my friends she didn't like, so I refused to tell her. *She got angry. Very, very angry.*

I sat on the kitchen couch while she screamed at me, saying: "Tell me. Tell me." Over and over. As her anger increased, I ground my teeth together and became more resistant. I refused to speak. My silence propelled her over to the cabinet that housed the wooden rolling pin. It was a long, fat piece of dark maple used to make filo dough. I knew what was coming. My mother always said her hands were too weak to beat me with, but the rolling pin wasn't.

Then, all I could hear was her screaming, "Why don't you tell me? Why do you hide things from me?"

I protected my head with my hands and curled up as much as possible. She hit me in many places, but the one that hurt the most was very high up on my inner thighs. I endured the beating silently. I didn't scream, cry, or say anything.

Because I showed no fear or weakness, it made her angrier. This time, she took things to the next level.

She told me to take off all of my clothes. I didn't want to, but I was in so much pain already, so I obeyed, wondering what she would do to me next. Then she told me those clothes were no longer mine and I didn't deserve to live there anymore.

"From now on, you will be on your own," she said.

She dragged me outside the kitchen, into the corridor, and down the stairs. She opened the door and locked me outside of our apartment, completely naked. I didn't know what to do or where to go. It was chilly and completely dark out. I decided to huddle close to the building near one of its corners. All I could think was: "What if someone sees me? What will they think about me or do to me?"

I didn't remember how long I was there, but I heard the third-floor neighbor open his front door at one point. I panicked. It was a tiny building, and he could get to the door where I was hiding in no time. Should I go out on the street and hide in the neighbor's building? Or I could run to our backyard and hide in the vegetable garden. Neither of these were good options. Either the neighbor would find me, or someone else would see me.

I guess my mother heard him, too. Because we lived on the first floor, she managed to beat him down the stairs. She opened the door and told me to get inside. I don't remember what happened after, but for weeks, I had a big, painful, dark purple bruise between my thighs.

Later, I asked her: "Why did you give birth to me if you hate me so much?"

"I don't hate you," she said. "I just want you to become a good person."

FRUSTRATED

When I was a little girl, when my mom was angry at me, she would beat me. I felt that it was unfair. I thought she was just angry, and I was the emotional outlet for her anger. That made me feel like she didn't want me. I felt deeply rejected.

After each of her anger episodes—each beating, or punishment, or each time she would scream at me—I felt so hurt, so unwanted, so frustrated, and confused that the only thing I wanted to do was to turn that pain and frustration towards myself. After all, I was only a powerless child; what else could I do?

And so I would go to my room, sit on my dark brown wood floor, curl up like a ball with my arms around my knees, and bang the back of my head into the cold brick wall covered only by wallpaper decorated on green leaf motifs. It hurt, but also felt good. There was something enjoyable in feeling my brain shake. And the more painful it became, the calmer I became. It felt like I was transferring all of my emotional pain and frustration to the wall.

The only problem was that sometimes she was in the other room, and she would hear me banging my head and come in to yell at me or beat me even more. So, I would have to figure out ways to punish myself. Out of frustration and desperation, I came up with the idea of beating my head into my knees or just hitting it with my hands. Unfortunately, this was not enough pain to do the trick.

Sometimes, I took it to the next level. In my rage against mistreatment, I would go into the bathroom (which had a lock) and pull out my hair. It felt good. Painful, yes, but getting rid of all that hair felt like I was getting rid of parts of myself. The more hair I could get into my hands, the more relaxed I became. It was all in hopeless desperation that this miserable life might end soon. When my mom saw the handfuls of beautiful, shiny, blond hair in the bathroom garbage bin, she would get even angrier and beat my fragile, innocent body again. Why? Why did I deserve this, I thought? Why am I living? Who are those people who want to hurt me so much? Was it just to beat me that she had me?

I wanted to die. If I could, I would have killed myself there and then. But I was too young and didn't know how. Once, I even told her out loud that I would kill myself, but of course, I got more punishment for it.

Sometimes, I wondered if people have kids to have a convenient outlet for their emotional frustration.

PUNISHED

One time, I took my father's cigarette lighter. It was a very beautiful and well-made lighter shaped like a little gun. It was plated in nice shiny chrome, and there were handmade engravings on the handle. Someone gave it to him as a present from a foreign country. I took it just to play with it and show it to my friends.

When he noticed the missing lighter, my father asked me if I had taken it. I got scared that he would punish me, so I told him that I didn't. He said that no one else had been around it, and I was the only one who could have taken it, but I persisted with my lie.

I remember him looking everywhere for it without any luck. That was because I had already hidden it in a big pile of snow shoved off the entrance pathway that had accumulated throughout the winter.

Time passed by, I forgot all about it. Then, the spring came.

One day, my father told me that he had finally found the lighter in the front yard. He asked me if I knew anything about it, and I said I didn't. He said there was no way the lighter could have gotten there by itself, but I still insisted on my lie. All he wanted me to do was admit I had taken it, but I didn't dare. I knew punishment was coming one way or another, so what was the point of admitting? He told my mother about it, and they decided to use the corner method.

They told me to stand up by the door, which separated the room from the corridor. Because I had lied, I would have to face the door corner, but this time, they were upset enough about my behavior to change the punishment.

First, they told me to put some old newspapers on the floor. Then they brought a pack of lentils from the kitchen and told me to open it and spread it out. I would have to go on my knees. It was excruciating. I was thinking that a beating would be better, but my father never beat me or hit me. That's why he decided to create something harrowing without touching me.

While on my knees, my mother read a book, and my father watched TV. They pretended I didn't exist. *I wanted to scream, but I didn't. I wanted to cry, but I didn't.* The only thing that helped me to take my mind off of the excruciating pain in my knees was carefully observing the door hinges. I explored every little detail in them. They were rusted, and the door trim around them was unevenly cut and badly painted. The wallpaper was also unevenly cut, and instead of the trim being on top, it was the other way around. I discovered there was so much to see in twenty centimeters from that corner.

I don't remember how long they made me stay like that, but it was long enough to feel endless. My knees were burning, and I remember hearing one of their voices tell me I could get up but remain facing the corner. I never liked to show weakness, so I tried to pretend it was not a big deal. In truth, I had a difficult time moving. The pain ran all through my legs. They were shaking. I couldn't feel my knees. I wanted to scream.

More time passed, and my only escape was to look deeper into the little details in the wall. Finally, my mother told me to clean up the lentils and the newspaper and to go to my room.

The corner method was a tough one. It tested my will, but I always stayed strong. I never showed weakness. But that didn't stop them from punishing me.

REPRESSED

When I was about ten years old, I decided I wanted to be a singer, so I signed up with a singing group at school. I remember going into the room where the class was being held, and the teacher told me to stand towards the back of the group. I felt comfortable there; I never liked being in the front. The song we sang first was one I knew, so there were no lyrical surprises. Singing in a group felt good because I wasn't the focus of attention.

I remember singing and hearing other kids singing and wishing I could be as good as them one day. Being part of that group made me feel like I had a voice for the first time. A voice that wants to be heard. It was so liberating.

Eventually, we even went to perform in the small local theatre. Dressed in traditional Bulgarian folk attire, seeing the audience and feeling their interest in us was interesting. It felt like we were doing something for the people. I found myself thinking that I wanted to sing all my life.

However, one day, shortly after the concert, I found myself signed out of my singing group. Of course, my mother had the power to do anything she wanted with me. When I asked her why, she said singing was not for me and I would not get anywhere in life with it. I was crushed.

Next, I decided I wanted to dance. I was not really into Bulgarian folklore, but since the only dancing group in the small town where my family lived was local folk dancing, I had no other choice. My first class was the beginner's class, where I had to learn the basic steps. The teacher briefly showed us the basics. I noticed that everyone was better than me, but I was determined to catch up with them. After learning the music track and the steps, we learned our first "horo". Horo is a Bulgarian communal dance performed for enjoyment, gatherings, and celebrations. The horo has a variety of moods and is danced in linked circles, serpentine chains, and straight lines.

Moving and holding hands with other students was a liberating group experience. I was so happy to find a positive outlet for my energy.

After a couple of weeks, my nose started running a bit. That was normal because it was winter, but one night after dancing, my mother said this would be my last class. I was shocked. When I asked why, she said: "This is how sickness starts. You must have gotten sweaty during the dance and now have a cold. If you continue to go, you will get much worse. I don't have time to take care of you."

I wanted to rebel and say that this was not the reason I had a runny nose and that I really wanted to dance, but what was the point? She had the power. To finalize her decree, she added that I couldn't miss school because of some stupid dancing.

I curled up on the couch to feel better but couldn't bring myself to do anything. Finally, I ground my teeth, got up, and left the room. In my bedroom, I cried and cried. I had no money to continue going and paying for the classes, and I was sure she would find a way to stop me even if I tried. Broken, sad, and disappointed, I went to bed.

The same happened with my attempt to paint and draw: "This is not for you," she said. "It is not useful for anything in life and is just a waste of time. You need a normal education and a profession to be a productive member of society and support yourself."

The last self-expression I tried was starting a journal. Putting my thoughts and feelings into words was a liberating outlet. I kept the journal in a safe place, under my mattress and away from everyone. I even made two holes in the book's hardcovers and put a lock on it (they didn't sell journals with locks back then in Bulgaria).

A week later, while I was in the kitchen with my mother, she asked me about something she couldn't have known or guessed without reading my journal. She also mentioned that I shouldn't keep secrets from her.

How could she invade my privacy? I felt so naked and unsafe about the violation that on the very next day, while she was working, I went out onto the balcony of our apartment and burned my journal in a tin bucket. While I watched it burn, I clearly remember telling myself that I would never write down any of my thoughts and feelings again.

FROZEN

Back in 1986 in Bulgaria, there was a TV show called *"Ne se surdi choveche"*. The English name of that game is *"Sorry"*. Usually, the best two classes from the top schools were invited to go and compete. One year, our class made the grade.

To prepare for the show, we had to study different subjects. It was challenging, but everyone studied a lot so that we could win. The main subjects were photography and history. My parents, being geography teachers, ensured I knew everything required.

We were sixth-grade students, and the competitors were in seventh grade. Seated on the opposite sides of the room, with the giant plastic dice between us, everyone was nervous. We were separated into four groups, and I was in the first one. I was number three. I hoped the host wouldn't throw that number, but he did, and I thought I would die.

I got up and headed down towards the stage. It seemed like a long way to get there. Almost visibly shaking, I stood behind the microphone and looked ahead. I heard the question they asked me, and all I could think was, why were all those lights in front of my face? I couldn't see anything—just bright white light. I could feel everyone's attention on me. It was overwhelming. I couldn't breathe. It was like I was naked, and my mind just went blank.

Then, the next thing I remember, I was back in my seat, wondering what just happened. I felt like I'd just woken up from a dream. Shocked, embarrassed, and speechless, it turned out I froze. I didn't answer the question. I didn't say anything. They had to replace me with another person so they could continue with the game. Luckily, the show was not broadcast live.

Later on the bus going home, I thought: "What will my mother say about this? How will she punish me? This was the ultimate embarrassment." Not only did I feel awful, but I felt like I let her down. At that point, I was prepared for anything. Whatever she was going to do would be fine with me. I felt like I deserved to be punished.

I had a massive headache at home and was exhausted from the long day. The feeling of shame was tremendous. Of course, my parents already knew what had happened. I couldn't imagine seeing their faces. I got in and went straight to my room, hoping for a way to forget everything.

While lying in bed and staring at the ceiling, my mother came in. Afraid of what she might say or do, I just remained quiet. She sat next to me on the corner of my bed and spoke in a soft voice.

"I know what happened," she said. My heart started forcing blood towards my head, and I felt like I was failing her all over again. But then she said: "Don't worry. Sometimes things happen. I'm not mad."

I couldn't believe my ears. Why wasn't she mad at me? She didn't yell or punish me in any way. She didn't even forbid me to do anything. What happened? Was that even her?

To this day, I don't have an explanation for her reaction that night.

COMMUNISM

I grew up during the communist regime in Bulgaria, which began in 1944. At the time, I thought we had everything. Free health care, including dental. Free education, including university. There was no unemployment, and there were (in theory) no social classes. Most of the working-class people had similar incomes, and every family had a house or an apartment that they owned. Material things like furniture, TVs, clothes, etc., were pretty much the same in every household. Everyone had to work and get a job that paid enough to live an everyday life. There was very little crime and no homeless people on the streets. It looked like a pretty good system.

However, there were several problems. A family was only allowed to have one apartment and a country house. People couldn't move freely from one place to another, even within the country, and they required special permits for relocation. People couldn't travel abroad, except to other communist countries, and then only with reason and special permission. With few exceptions, people couldn't emigrate or work abroad.

We also feared to speak or express anything other than communist views. All we could watch on TV and listen to on the radio were socialist news, movies, or shows. Every Friday at 8 pm, instead of the news block from Sofia, we had to watch the news block of the USSR TV, which was broadcast directly from Moscow in Russian. Russian was the first foreign language taught at school; English was the last. We had to wait many years to get a car, and it had to be one that was produced in a communist country. We saw bananas, tangerines, and oranges only once a year, just before New Year, and we couldn't buy more than a certain amount.

Religious organizations were restrained or banned. The Christian Orthodox Church of Bulgaria continued functioning, but the communist functionaries assumed many high roles within the church. No member of the communist party or its affiliations was allowed to enter any church. During the religious holidays, assigned members of the communist party patrolled in front of the Churches to see who was attending. If they saw a member of the party, he or she would be in trouble.

The communist party operated three youth organizations. The first was *"Chavdarche"*. These were the youngest children, from 6 years to 9 years old. They had to wear a sky-blue scarf. The second was *"Pioneri"*. These were the older children from 9 to 14 years old. They wore red scarves. The third was *"Komsomol"*, from 14 to up to 28 years old. Participation in those organizations was obligatory, especially for those planning to enter higher education like a university, where *"Komsomol"* reference characteristics were essential for acceptance.

My mother always used to tell me: "Be careful what you say and to whom you say it because you never know what might happen. Someone could be a friend to you today, but maybe not tomorrow. Never trust anyone."

I went to school every day wearing a mandatory uniform and a blue or red scarf, which I hated so much that I chewed the end while sitting in class. I forgot my scarf at home a few times, and the teachers standing at the school entrances wouldn't let me in. No scarf, no school. I would have loved to skip school, but my mother would have made my life difficult.

When this happened for the first time, I panicked. I didn't know what to do. I couldn't miss any classes. At that time, my mother was still the principal of my school, which was terrible for me. I couldn't skip classes just like that. Especially not because I forgot my scarf! *What kind of an example was I to show to others?*

Then, I got creative. I went around the back side of the building, where I saw a friend standing by the window. I asked her to borrow her scarf. She dropped it for me, and I could enter and avoid missing the classes. This saved me from the lecture at home and who knows what else!

Back then, I just accepted everything as normal. *Those were the rules, and that was life.* I didn't know any different — for better or worse.

CHERNOBYL

On April 26, 1986, the Chernobyl Nuclear Disaster struck the former Soviet Union. This was by far the worst catastrophe in the history of nuclear energy but in Communist Bulgaria, it was hidden from the public. Covering up the truth about the disaster and taking no measures to protect the population solely for the purpose of protecting the high party leadership was one of the most significant crimes committed by the Bulgarian communist regime.

Not counting the three Soviet republics of Ukraine, Belarus, and Russia, Bulgaria ranked fifth in terms of the degree of radioactive pollution following the Chernobyl Disaster. However, regarding adequate radiation exposure during the first year after the incident, Bulgaria ranked first. That was due to the cover-up preventing Bulgaria's population from taking even the most basic precautions. Ironically, on May 1st, mandatory Labor Day parades were held in Bulgaria's large cities under the falling radioactive rain. When the authorities finally told us about the disaster, they presented it as something casual and not at all dangerous.

Instead of going to the mandatory parade that year, my sister, her best girlfriend, and I decided to rebel and visit my father's parents and relatives in a town called Kazanlak, which is located in the center of the country. We made two cakes, got clothes, and headed to the car. It was raining, and my sister had to drive with extra care. I don't remember the details of our Labor Day celebration, but I remember that on the next day, we ate a lot of lettuce. My grandparents had a little vegetable garden, and they said it seemed like the lettuce doubled overnight.

Before we left to return home, our grandparents gave us all a few baskets full of lettuce. Enough to last ten days. On our way home, my sister's friend and I ate lettuce and talked in the car.

She said: "I have never seen such a big lettuce. It is so delicious."

"Yes," I said. "Maybe grandma and grandpa watered it more or added extra fertilizer."

Then my sister said: "I don't feel well. I feel sleepy."

"Maybe you should pull over and get some coffee," her friend said.

"I don't feel well, too," I said. "I feel nauseous."

She pulled over as soon as she could. I got out of the car and immediately threw up.

My sister went to get some coffee to continue driving while I wondered why I got sick. She always drove very carefully, and this was the first time I got nauseous while driving.

A few days later, my sister learned about some people taking precautions and placing wet towels in front of their doors. Others were taking iodine. She realized the government was not telling us the truth and that the fact that we got sick two days after the radioactive rain was not a coincidence. That lettuce was a poison. She took the basket and dumped its contents in the garbage outside. Unfortunately, we never took any iodine. Nor did we realize that not only all of the fresh food but even the water had been contaminated.

DEATH

On that same May 1st, 1986, my grandma was walking down the streets of Sofia on her way to my aunt's apartment to celebrate with her and her family. She got soaking wet in the rain because she forgot to bring an umbrella. She was a strong, healthy 70-year-old woman. A month later, she felt sick and visited her doctor. They performed lab tests for lung cancer, but the results were negative. By the end of August, she was struggling to walk and spent most of her time at home in bed.

My mother decided to send me to visit my grandma twice a day: once in the morning and once in the afternoon. We all knew she was dying, but at twelve years old, I didn't fully understand what that meant. Mom said she was sending me instead of going herself because I was faster with my bicycle, although my grandma's house was only ten minutes away on foot. Twice a day, I would try to make my grandma eat something healthy; it broke my heart to see her so lifeless. Eventually, all she would eat were a few chocolate bonbons, which she threw up shortly after.

One morning after breakfast, my mother said: "Why don't you go and see how your grandma is doing?" As usual, I rode my white *"Balkan"* bicycle. I remember it was a beautiful sunny September day, but I felt uneasy during the ride. In a few minutes, I arrived at my grandma's house. I left my bike in the backyard, opened the front door, and went inside.

I walked along the corridor to her bedroom door, opened it, and slipped inside. The curtains were closed, and I could barely see anything coming in from the bright outside.

"Grandma?" I said, "Grandma, how are you?"

There was no reply. Slowly, I drew closer to her bedside. My heart beat so loudly and fast that I couldn't hear anything else. I asked again: "Grandma? Can you hear me?"

At last, my eyes adjusted to the light. I now stood right beside her. She was lying still with her eyes closed and her mouth slightly open. It was so quiet in her room that I could tell she wasn't breathing. I continued to listen, but there was nothing. I began to tremble. I didn't know what to do. I wanted to start crying but couldn't. A big ball of sorrow was stuck in my throat. I wanted to touch her, but I got scared and ran out of the house and rode my bike back home as fast as possible.

Still shaking, I went straight to the kitchen, where my mother was washing dishes, and said, "Grandma is not breathing."

Without stopping her activity, she just asked me if I was sure.

"Yes," I said. "I'm sure. I called her a few times, and there was no answer."

Looking at my mother, I found it strange that she continued washing the dishes. How is it possible for her not to react? I thought. Didn't she love her mother?

I continued watching her, unable to move. After she finished all the dishes, she wiped her hands and, with an icy and monotonous voice, said that she needed to change and go to my grandma's house. I stayed at home. When she came back, she confirmed that my grandma was dead. It was September 9th, just a little over four months after the Chernobyl disaster.

The final diagnosis of death was lung cancer, though she never smoked a cigarette in her whole life.

I loved my grandmother very much. She was always nice to me and never beat me or did anything abusive at all.

AFRICA

My parents wanted to make more money and, after intensively studying Portuguese, were accepted to work in Angola as adult teachers. Because my grandma was no longer alive, no one could take care of me, so they decided that I should join them. My sister, who was ten years older than me, stayed in Bulgaria.

My first trip outside of the country was on my own. I was scared. It was also my first time on an airplane. I was twelve years old, speaking only Bulgarian and Russian. From Sofia to Luanda, I had a connecting flight in Rome. Luckily, there were other Bulgarians who were going on the same route. They were kind to me and helped me out with the basics. They told me the flight would be delayed and helped me find the gate. I liked Rome's airport. It had so many people and stores with shiny things in them. I thought, "Why is it different in Sofia?"

When we landed in Luanda, my father was waiting for me. The first thing I noticed after getting off the plane was that I couldn't breathe. The humidity was so high that I could only sip a little air.

After spending one night in the Bulgarian worker's building, we took another plane for M'banza-Kongo. That is the capital of Angola, northwestern Zaire Province, where my parents had been sent to work.

I looked out of the plane window during our descent.

Between the lush green vegetation and palm trees, many houses were made out of dirt, grass, and a bit of water with metal roofs. My father explained that the people living in those houses slept on the floor on small grass beds, and when the rainy season came, their homes would sometimes flood, and they would have no place to sleep. It seemed so sad to have to live like that, I thought. As the plane landed, I saw dozens of kids running alongside the runway, smiling and waving at us. My father explained they were happy to see planes landing and taking off. I thought running next to a big plane like that must be dangerous.

On my first weekend in Angola, my father thought it would be a great idea if he took me to the local farmer's market. The first thing we bought was a pineapple. I had never seen a pineapple before. He explained that it's a tropical fruit that grows as a shrub close to the ground. Then he said: "It's too crowded. You stay here, and I'll get the rest of the necessary things."

In no time, I was surrounded by people. They made a circle around me and were coming closer and closer toward me. I started to hear my heart in my ears, and it was loud. As the circle around me got smaller, some people started touching my bare arms. They were saying the word *"Branca"* over and over. What will they do to me? I thought. I remember reading stories about cannibal natives who made sacrifices for the explorers. Would they eat me?

Unable to do anything, I was frozen. Their voices got louder, and I could barely breathe or move from the closeness. Some people were barely touching my skin like they would get burned, and some were pushing their fingers deep into my flesh. I wanted the earth to open so I could fall and disappear. Where is my father? I thought. Why did he leave me alone?

After a while, I saw people moving from my left side. Suddenly, I heard my father saying something. It took some more time until I saw his face and felt his hand grabbing mine and dragging me out of the circle. I was safe.

ACCIDENT

On Valentine's Day, 1987, my father asked me if I wanted to go to the beach with him. I enjoyed going to the beach, and even though I feared the water, I said, "Yes." My mother decided to stay home.

Our car was parked on the street in front of our 22-story building, where only Bulgarian workers lived. The car was a famous Russian brand called Lada. My parents were thrilled to have that car because, in Bulgaria, they could never have afforded such a luxury. Not only was it too expensive, there was a waiting list to buy it.

As always, I sat in the back seat. But this time my father said: "You don't have to sit on the back. This is not Bulgaria. Come up and sit in the front."

I hesitated but decided that it would be more fun up front. When I reached for the seatbelt, he said. "You don't have to put on your seatbelt. This is not Bulgaria. No one will give us a ticket for that here."

At the beach, my father and I had a pleasant time. Even though I couldn't swim, I enjoyed sunbathing. He rarely spent time with me, so I was extremely happy we were together. After a few hours, we had enough of the sun and decided to go home. I sat in the front seat on my way back, too. Five minutes later, I remember seeing a big car swerve in front of us, and the next thing I knew, I was standing outside in a daze.

I don't remember how I got out of the car, but my first memory is looking down at my clothes and seeing a lot of blood on my beautiful white T-shirt. It was one of my favorite shirts, with unusual Asian symbols. My first thought was: "My mother will be mad at me. How am I going to wash the blood? I love this shirt." I decided I needed to wash it as soon as possible so there wouldn't be any stains. Where was all this blood coming from anyway?

Then, I felt an excruciating pain in my left wrist. It swelled up so fast that I thought the bones must have been smashed. Dissociated and disoriented, I finally looked at our car. It was so badly mangled that it looked like there was no front to it. The windshield was cracked and covered in blood. When I came closer, I saw some hair along with the blood. It was my hair.

The other car was a big Safari Land Rover, which didn't show much damage. Then, there was a lot of chaos I don't remember, but eventually, my father and I found ourselves in the back of the Land Rover. I was in shock, and my face was burning. When my mother saw us, she became hysterical and started crying. I told her: "Don't worry! The most important thing is that we are alive."

At the hospital, the Russian doctors put a few stitches in my father's lower lip, which he had hit on the steering wheel. Other than the bruises on his arms and chest, he was fine. On the other hand, they diagnosed me with a skull fracture, concussion, and a broken arm. For me, the worst part was that my face had little cuts over it, some of which were pretty bad. Apparently, I broke the windshield with my head before falling between the dashboard and the seat.

Because of the concussion, I had to stay home for a month and not read, write, or do anything that would make my brain work. It was a long month where I laid in bed all day looking at the ceiling fan and, from time to time, scratching my cast-covered, itchy arm with a metal shish.

For a few weeks, my parents didn't allow me to see my face. I wanted to cry when I saw it in the mirror for the first time. There were cuts everywhere. On my forehead, brows, and mouth, but the worst was my nose. The top part of it was unevenly half-cut, and it looked like I had two big pimples that would stay there forever. *What will I do now? No one is going to like me?*

Most of the scars on my face healed, but some are still visible. My father never apologized for making me sit in the front without a seatbelt.

ILLUSION

Visiting a capitalist country during Bulgaria's communist regime was not something everyone got to experience. Traveling outside the "iron curtain" was usually forbidden. The only reason my parents and I could go to Italy at all was because our flights to Africa usually connected in Rome.

I clearly remember my first time. Walking on the streets of this ancient city had a profound impact on me. The cultural shock of seeing stores and markets overflow with so many different varieties of foods and goods was overwhelming for me.

My parents were very generous and told me I could buy any toy. I got so excited. I wanted one of those hand-held electronic video game players. That wasn't something we could get in Bulgaria. They took me to a store filled with all kinds of electronic games and gadgets. Everywhere I looked, there was more. The shelves were stocked from floor to ceiling.

My parents asked me which one I wanted. But I couldn't answer. All I could think was: Wow! How am I going to choose?

I just froze, so they randomly picked one, handed it to me, and asked: "Do you want this one?"

I still couldn't answer. It was all too much for me. I stood there for a while in shock and confusion and then told them I wanted to go. We left the store empty-handed.

Later, while we were walking the small streets in the ancient town, I was struck by vivid memories of our surroundings. All that caught my eye felt like a *déjà vu*. I remember thinking that I used to live there. I saw familiar old buildings, windows, balconies, and doors wherever I gazed. I glanced between my feet, and even the paving stones appeared recognizable. I knew every corner of every rock on the buildings and the street.

Something in me told me to look to the left, across the street. There was a window with some clothes wire in front of it. Where are the flower baskets? I thought. There used to be nutmeg red flowers there.

In this strange moment of surprise, excitement, and happiness, I told my mother: "Mom, I used to live here."

She laughed at me and said, "There is no way you could have lived here. Maybe it was a dream you had."

"But you don't understand," I replied. "I remember living here. I recognize everything. I know the windows and the doors, everything!"

She then changed the subject. It was clear that she didn't believe me. I was crushed, but I continued to admire the surroundings quietly. When we had to leave the street, it felt like saying goodbye to an old friend. I wish I remembered its name so I could go there again one day.

On our last day, I sat on one of the benches at the airport, waiting for the plane to Sofia. Everything looked so lovely, so polished, so beautiful. People were different: smiling and polite. The picture painted in our minds by the communist government greatly contrasted with what I saw. I asked my parents why we didn't live there, and they said it was forbidden. I didn't dare say anything, but this was the moment I decided to one day leave Bulgaria.

That first visit to the eternal city shifted my world and my perspective. The hunger to see different places, experience different cultures, and taste other foods still burns within me.

INDOCTRINATED

Both of my parents were teachers and school principals. Being schooled all the time was my existence. If I tried to rebel, I was punished. They always reminded me about their positions and that I needed to be an example for others.

At school, we had to look as neat as possible—clean and very much put together with uniforms and white collars. The guys couldn't have long hair. The girls couldn't have long nails or any nail polish or makeup. Anything that would make you stand out from the crowd was forbidden.

Once, I put on a clear coat of nail polish. I thought no one at school would notice, but I was wrong.

When my math teacher saw it, she said: "Why are you wearing nail polish, Borislava?"

I answered: "But it's almost invisible."

Because I showed bravery and character, she got mad. She commanded me to get up, go to the blackboard, and resolve a math equation in front of the class. I responded with further rebellion. Instead of solving the problem, I stood before the blackboard, doing nothing. This made my teacher so mad that in front of all the students in the class, she said: "I know you can finish the equation. You are not solving it on purpose. I know that your mother is a principal in one of the most elite schools in Sofia, and your father is a principal, too. Did they teach you to behave like that? I will make sure they learn about that. I'll give you an "F," which will lower your final grade and make it difficult for you to apply for university. Now get out of the class".

Why was she so evil? What was so wrong with clear nail polish?

Going home after that incident was not easy. I remember walking with my girlfriend and discussing what would happen next. I knew my parents would be upset. I knew things were about to get even more difficult for me. What could I have done, I thought? It started from a nail polish and exploded to a lower final grade. *Why? What was wrong with the whole picture?*

At home, my parents were furious. My mother yelled at me: "Why were you wearing nail polish? You know it's forbidden! Why didn't you obey the teacher? What are you going to do with a B grade now? You won't be able to apply to any University, and you will become a low-level medical nurse because only they have job openings in this stagnant economy! Do you want to carry urine trays around all day? If no University accepts you, that's what you are going to do!"

The list of insulting suggestions about my future went on and on, and I just sat there and took it. Their final verdict was that I had to ask the teacher for an extra exam to improve my grade. I felt so bad because of the lack of support or understanding. Just the thought of going to that math class again was making me feel sick to my stomach.

Nervrtheless, I spoke with the teacher. I apologized and asked for an extra exam. She told me that because of the apology, she would make an exception and allow me to do this. But even though I got an "A" on that exam, my final grade was still a "B."

REVOLUTION

The Communist regime started collapsing in 1989 and finally fell in 1990 when I was sixteen years old.

I remember watching the TV and seeing all those people protesting in front of the parliament. There was a new protest song: *"This Time Is Ours,"* that was saying: *"45 Years Are Enough,"* and wishing for a new life where the people, not the regime, would determine their own destiny. Everything felt like living in a movie—the same people with the same beliefs trying to live differently.

Two of the immediate changes affecting me were the removal of teachers guarding the school entrance and the requirement to wear scarves and school uniforms. I could even wear denim if I wanted—something that had been unthinkable before. I could wear make-up and nail polish with any color I wanted. At last, I felt like I could breathe. I had found a way to express myself.

Our access to television changed dramatically as well. There were suddenly more than the two programs controlled and influenced by the Bulgarian Communist party-run government. We could watch many foreign films and TV series. Cable and satellite television also became available. I had a TV in my room and started watching it day and night, absorbing anything I could. My favorite channel was

MTV Europe. I remember admiring the artists and the videos and wondering how people could be so open and liberated.

During the transition, the stores became empty. There was nothing to buy. Unlike others, our family didn't have any living relatives in the villages that could provide us with some meat, eggs, or milk. We relied only on what they would supply the stores with.

Every day, my parents would wake me up at 5 am and send me to the local store. There, I had to wait in a long line of people who woke up earlier than me and were already there. We didn't know what we would buy with the coupons we purchased with money. It didn't matter. As long as they had something that day, it was good. Bread, milk, sugar, flour, or something else. Anything looked like gold on those empty shelves. Depending on the family size, our family of four was allowed to buy only one loaf of bread and milk a day.

In addition to all this, Bulgaria started seeing criminality like never before. The police were not prepared to care about and control crime, which back then had been kept low through fearful methods. This included all levels, from the robbery of household possessions to the mass theft of capital, machinery, materials, and even furniture from industry and institutions. As a result, many factories failed and were closed.

Very soon, Bulgaria was not safe anymore. The mafia was born and rapidly rose to power. I felt increasingly uncomfortable and helpless and wanted to leave the country.

DISCOURAGED

Right after graduating high school, I signed up for driving lessons. In Bulgaria, such classes were mandatory for applying for a license. Two exams followed a course competition—one written exam covering theory and the other a practical driving exam with the instructor and a police officer in the back seat. I passed the theory immediately but had to take the driving test twice because I failed on the first try. It was early winter by the time of my exam, and it was not easy driving stick shift in snowy conditions where the streets were not clean, and there was ice under the snow.

Proud of my new driver's license and achievement during such harsh weather conditions, I asked my father if I could drive his car. He told me he couldn't let me do that during the winter, but he promised to give it to me in the spring.

When spring arrived, I thought it would be nice to borrow his car to practice and not forget everything.

But my father said, "How can I give you the car when you are going to have an accident on the first turn." Then he pointed out the window and showed me the intersection with the tree I would crash into. I was disappointed and complained to my mother about it. She said that he was scared because of our car accident together, and that was why he was so resistant.

"But I passed my test on the busy streets of Sofia, and this is a small town with barely any cars on the street," I said. She agreed but didn't want to confront him.

A month later, I tried again. This time, he said he would give it to me only if he sat next to me for the first couple of times. I told him I already had a license and this was not necessary, but he refused to let me drive without him. In the end, I agreed because I had no other choice.

My father's car was an East German Wartburg. It was a fascinating creation with a 3-cylinder engine, a gear stick on the steering column, and the requirement to mix oil with petrol to lubricate the engine. The transmission was equipped with a freewheel, with no need to engage the clutch between gears.

It was a sunny early afternoon day. My father and I got into the car and put on our seat belts. We had learned our lesson. I started the engine and activated the first gear. Then, I slowly started to drive. At the first intersection (the one he said I would crush into), I stopped to look out for cars. After I made sure it was safe, I turned right. I continued to drive on the same road without seeing any other vehicles. Two minutes later, we came to a slight downhill and another intersection with a stop sign. Going downhill, I started pressing the brake a little to reduce the speed. Suddenly, my father pulled the hand break between us and stopped the car.

"Why did you do that?" I asked.

"You were going way too fast." he said, "and you wouldn't be able to stop at the stop sign."

I disagreed, saying that I already started stopping, and we were more than fifty meters away, which gave us more than enough time to stop.

"No," he said. "You wouldn't be able to stop. You were going to have an accident with another car at the intersection."

I got so mad that I turned off the engine, opened my car door, and got out.

Walking back home, I was angry and crying with pain in my heart. Why was he so unfair? I thought. Why doesn't he let me do anything? Was it because he loved his car so much and didn't want to give it to anyone else? But he allowed my sister to drive it. Why not me? Why does he hate me? Why didn't they encourage me to do anything besides study?

Back home, my mother was waiting for me. Because my father had come home earlier, she knew what had happened. Then she said: "You both are very stubborn. That is why you don't get along."

I didn't see how this had anything to do with what had just happened, and his behavior was still hurtful and unacceptable, but he kept silent. *I was tired of fighting.*

I never asked to drive his precious car again.

UNIVERSITY

After graduating from high school, I had to apply to the University. I had no idea what to study. At that time, I was into fashion and spent every moment I had drawing different outfits. I enjoyed it but received no support from my family. They wanted me to become a teacher just like them. It gave me chills to picture myself as someone who would make other people miserable, just like they and my school teachers were making me miserable.

During that time, I started dating my first boyfriend. He was not the type of guy my parents liked. Basically, he was a bad boy who wanted to fight with other bad boys, was a few years older than me, and had not-so-good grades at school. He worked as a DJ at the local nightclub, where I liked dancing. Even though I was just 17, I was out every night. Dancing in the club was my outlet. I even started helping my boyfriend at one point by mixing songs recorded on audio cassettes. It was so much fun, but my parents hated it. They wanted me to focus on studying.

When my mother saw me becoming this wild and difficult-to-control teenager, she made an extra effort each day to sit and help me study. One of her University majors was geography, and she said it would be easy for her to teach me that required material.

Honestly, I didn't care. I hated all of it, and the only thing I could think about was the evening when I would see my boyfriend, mix music, and dance to *Depeche Mode.*

My parents made me apply to two Universities. The first was the *University of Sofia,* and the second was the *University of National and World Economy,* also in Sofia. Day after day, my mother repeated the materials and drilled me with questions to test my memory. It was challenging to remember things I didn't care about, so I constantly wrote down the most important things. It was the only way I could remember them. Then came the day of the first exam.

On the way there, I remember having a big knot of pain in my stomach. I could barely breathe. At the exam, I wrote what I could remember and left when the time was up. Later, I would take the exam at the second university with the same discomfort and nervousness.

A few weeks after the second exam, the results from the *University of Sofia* came out. My father was so anxious that he went there early in the morning to see if I had been accepted. To his disappointment, he found out that I had been disqualified.

He came home angry and asked me: "What did you do? They only disqualify people who are cheating. Did you cheat?"

"No," I told him. "I didn't do anything."

Then he said, "There must be a reason. Get dressed, and let's go to find out what happened."

We spoke to a counselor and discovered that I had written my name on the top of the exam paper. *Unbelievable!* He was shocked.

I was shocked. All the applications were anonymous, and doing something like that immediately disqualified me.

"Did you do the same thing with your other application?" he asked, and I said I didn't remember. I had been way too stressed to remember anything. My parents were heartbroken.

A week later, while I was still sleeping, my parents entered my room with excitement in their eyes. They said my father had just returned from the *University of National and World Economy* and saw that I'd been accepted. Never before had I seen them so happy. I thought that if they were pleased, I must also be satisfied. I'm going to study accounting and auditing now. At least I won't be a teacher.

SUICIDE

There was tremendous pressure from my family to leave my boyfriend and focus on my studies. My mother got depressed because she didn't like him, and my father even had a conversation with me, which was rare. He told me that being with that guy was making her feel unwell and that if something happened to her physically, like a heart attack or something else, it would be my fault.

My sister and I moved into an apartment together in Sofia. That gave me a bit of relief, but I still felt like I had to break up with my boyfriend to make my parents happy. Meanwhile, studying accounting was something I really couldn't connect with. It was dry and dull. I wouldn't say I liked it. I had become miserable, lonely, and depressed. I couldn't see any way out. No one understood me. As days went by, I decided to finally end this constant pain and kill myself.

The thought that I would finally be free from this miserable life felt liberating. I had always hated my life to some degree. I always wondered why I was here or what the purpose of it all was. I just wanted it to end. Even though I knew that my family would be devastated, I couldn't imagine living like this anymore.

I'll never forget getting into the bathtub filled with warm water and placing a razor on the porcelain edge beside me. I felt very comfortable, hugged by the crystal-clear hot water. I took the razor in my right hand and started cutting the veins of my left wrist. I made three minor cuts, one next to another. The warm blood began to run and mixed with the hot water. Then, I took the razor with my left hand. I made three more cuts on my right wrist. The blood continued flowing. Then I put the razor on the side of the tub and submerged both of my arms in the water. The way my blood was coloring the water in the tub was beautiful. I closed my eyes and hoped it would be fast.

After a while, I realized it was strange that I still had my senses. I was starting to feel cold. I opened my eyes and looked into the water. It was pink but not red. I found that moving my fingers was easy as well. Then I lifted my hands out of the water, and to my vast surprise, I discovered that the blood had stopped flowing. I didn't understand why my attempt had been unsuccessful. The cuts were there, but my blood had stopped flowing.

Now what? I thought. Should I cut some more, or should I give up on this? My wrists hurt immensely, and the water was getting cold, so I quit.

A few days after my unsuccessful attempt, I tried again. This time, I took a large amount of sleeping pills. I went to bed with a smile on my face. I remember how happy I was that this struggle was going to end. To my surprise, however, I woke up—twenty-something hours later.

How is this possible? I thought. *Why can't I succeed in this?* Even in death, there isn't any fairness. Then I thought that maybe this was not the way out of this life. I decided to quit trying for a while and see what would happen.

No one ever found out that I tried to kill myself. My parents, sister, and relatives still don't know.

At the time, only one friend saw the bands around my wrists, but we didn't discuss it. It was during one of the cold winters in Bulgaria, and I could hide inside the long sleeves of pullovers and shirts.

Later in life, during some blood tests, I found out I have a rare condition where my veins will collapse and my blood will quickly stop flowing. My body goes into a "safe mode" and says, *I'll keep all of that blood to myself.*

PART TWO

TRANSITION

After I graduated from the University, I began to look for accounting jobs. This was during the transition to capitalism, which was a painful process because neither the government nor the people were ready for it. It involved the privatization of agricultural land, properties, and industry. Shares in the new system were issued to all citizens in the government enterprises. Because those industries were no longer tied with the Eastern Block nor competitive on the global market, the shift triggered mass unemployment.

I felt fortunate and thrilled to get a job as a cashier in a bank. The job turned out to be incredibly stressful because I worked with massive amounts of money and had to learn to distinguish real currencies from fake ones. To do so, I had to touch and examine every bill.

After a few months of this, I came down with a rash. It started from my hands and spread all over my arms, neck, and face. I went to a doctor who determined the rash was from handling currency. I was allergic to money. Everyone thought it was hilarious, and a few weeks later, they transferred me to the tellers' department.

During this time, the country experienced several episodes of drastic inflation and currency devaluation. I remember at one point, I was making the equivalent of $10 per month, which was a lot more than what my parents were making. Stores were empty, and for lunch, I was having a "sandwich with nothing," as I called it. It was basically two slices of bread with a bit of mayo and some ketchup. That's all. No meat, no cheese, nothing else. It was then that I decided to become more proactive and try my luck in another country.

A friend told me about the United States green card lottery, which anyone in Bulgaria could apply for. The requirements were to write your name and level of education, including a picture of yourself, and sign the form. I told my boyfriend Petar and all of my friends to apply. Then we waited.

Petar was offered an opportunity to work in Greece. One of his friends told him we could live in her family's summer house and work for a relative's business. We wouldn't have to pay any rent, so we could keep all of our earnings.

I hated my stressful job at the Bank, so at twenty-three years of age, I quit and joined my boyfriend on this new adventure.

The island where we lived was Crete, the largest island in Greece. A job was already waiting for us upon our arrival: to organize and pack Christmas Holiday gifts for one of the local sailing company employers. When Christmas came, our job switched to making wax candles and gluing labels on homemade honey jars for the tourists. After a few weeks of this, I got bored, so I quit and started looking for another, more exciting job. Something that would put my brain to better use.

Two weeks later, a friend of mine recommended me to a small rent-a-car family business, and they interviewed me for the job. The owners liked me and hired me right away. Renting cars for European tourists was something I felt comfortable with. After a month, I recommended my boyfriend. The owners hired him, too. It was good. We got to drive nice cars and have a good time.

Even so, we were starting to realize that we didn't want to stay and work in Greece. We would always be the immigrants from Bulgaria, and they were always going to look down on us. Our opportunities were minimal.

One day in the afternoon, while we were at the beach, Petar said he needed to tell me something. I could feel he was nervous. He told me that two days ago, his father had called and told him he had won the *US green card lottery*. I couldn't believe it. Happy, shocked, surprised! The lottery I made him apply for. I asked him what he wanted to do, and he said: "Let's get married and try our luck there." Even though that was not the proposal I was dreaming about, it felt like I was in heaven.

So, we took the money earned, packed up, and returned to Bulgaria. The plan was to get married and fill out the required immigration paperwork. Then, while waiting for the next step from the US Embassy, Petar would have to serve six months in the (back then) mandatory army, and I would study to improve my English in Bulgaria. It sounded like a great plan.

MARRIAGE

Back in Bulgaria, Petar and I felt lucky and excited. I told my parents we were getting married and my mother was thrilled because she loved my boyfriend very much. He was the unborn son she never had. I still think she loved him more than me.

Then we went to my boyfriend's parents to tell them about our decision. We got together in the living room of their house. I could feel the tension in the air but thought maybe they were just nervous. Petar started talking. He told them that we wanted to move forward with the immigration paperwork to move to America and that we wanted to go there together. To do that, we needed to get married as soon as possible before his six mandatory months in the army.

Abruptly, his father interrupted him and started yelling at us. "What do you think you will do in America? You will wash dishes. That's all. Why did you study so much? You are a doctor, and you should work as one here!"

I was in shock. I didn't expect this. Not only what I was hearing from his father but, most importantly, the fact that Petar wasn't saying anything in return.

"And why are you going to get married?" His father went on.

"Do you know who else got married that fast? Your uncle and you very well know what happened to him. He got divorced."

I wanted to say something here, but this was not my father. My body froze. I felt humiliated. *What am I doing here?* I thought. Why is Petar silent? Why is his mother quiet, too?

I don't remember how I got up and left, leaving all of them there, but I remember thinking I never wanted to feel embarrassed again.

At home, I didn't talk to anyone for a while, and then I told my parents that the immigration to America and the marriage plans were off. I guess I was going to look for another job. I spoke with Petar briefly before he went to serve in the army and told him about my disappointment in his inability to speak out to his father. I told him that we were over.

Seven months later, I found Petar waiting for me in front of my new office, where I was working as an accountant. He was holding a big bouquet. He told me he was delighted to see me and that he had a surprise for me. He suggested we go to a restaurant and talk. I was hesitant but agreed.

At the restaurant, he explained that he was sorry for all that happened. He said that his parents tried to find him a job, but because of the repressed economy, they were not successful. Eventually, they started coming to the idea of us getting married and going to the US.

I was stunned by his enthusiasm. He was acting like nothing had happened. All the humiliation and rejection I had received meant nothing to him. Upset but firm, I told him I didn't want to marry him because I couldn't forgive him. He cried and asked me to change my mind, but I refused.

A few days later, I saw my mother waiting for me, seated on the living room sofa in the apartment where my sister and I were living. She said she had come to spend the night with us, which she had never done before. After I changed my clothes and got comfortable, she told me Petar had visited her with a big bouquet. He wanted to talk to her, so she invited him in. He said to her that he hoped she could help us get married.

"I don't want to influence you," she said, "but everyone makes mistakes. He made one. So what? You should learn to forgive."

That night, I couldn't sleep. My mother was on the bed beside mine, and I could feel the pressure radiating from her even as she slept.

What should I do? I thought. If I don't get married, she will be disappointed in me. She liked him very, very much. Maybe she is right. Perhaps I should give him a second chance.

The very next day, I agreed to get married. A month later, we had a small wedding. Three months later, Petar and I were on our way to the United States of America.

IMMIGRATION

Arriving in a foreign land with a high standard of living and only $3000 in our pockets was no small challenge. On top of that, the language barrier was enormous, and we had to find jobs as soon as possible because a few thousand dollars wouldn't go far in Silicon Valley during the dot-com boom of 1999. The cheapest one-bedroom apartment we could find was $950 monthly plus a $500 deposit. In addition, we had to buy a car right away because the public transportation in the Bay Area is not something the country could be proud of. We bought an old stick-shift Mazda, which cost us another 850 dollars. Luckily, my husband knew a Bulgarian couple living in the area. They allowed us to stay with them for the first few weeks and connected us with people who could help us find jobs.

Petar got hired within the first week. On the twelfth day of our arrival, I got lucky and found a position as a sales associate at Macy's. I still don't know why they hired me. My English was terrible because I had given up hope of immigrating, and there was no time to study when it happened. At first, I felt highly uncomfortable at Macy's. I was very shy, but at that job, I had to talk with strangers in a language I could barely understand or speak. I quickly learned to escape from questions with some magic sentences: "Let me ask my co-worker. I'm new here." Then, leading the co-worker to the client,

I listened carefully to the rest of their conversation. Gradually, I discovered words like a turtleneck, overall, tank top, and brands like Calvin Klein, Tommy Hilfiger, and Esprit.

Trying to make it to two jobs in two different locations, with different schedules and only one car, was extremely stressful. One day, just a month after starting my job, I got into a car accident. The worst part is that it was my fault. I had been thinking of a million things we needed to do and didn't notice when the traffic light changed to red, and the car in front of me stopped suddenly. I slammed into her bumper.

When we pulled over and got out of our cars, I started crying and shaking. I didn't know what to do. The other driver was very sweet and tried to calm me down. She kept saying: "I'm sorry. Are you okay? Like it had been her fault and not mine."

Of course, the police came and wrote up a report. Her car was a new Lexus, and it took almost no damage, but our old Mazda's hood was folded up like an accordion and was no longer drivable. The policeman told me he would have to call for a tow. I freaked out. My body started trembling even more.

I couldn't stop it. Our friends told us that a tow would be a minimum of $200. I asked if I could leave the car in the nearby parking lot, and I guess he felt sorry for me because he agreed, but only until the end of the day. Then he offered to drive me home. Being at the back of a police car during the first month of immigration made me feel like I was in an American drama movie where no one knew how it was going to end.

When I told Petar about the car incident, he got aggressive and nasty. He started throwing things at me and yelling: "How could you do this? What will we do now? Do you know how much this is going to cost? Now I have to call the insurance and deal with that because you don't speak English."

The list of insults went on and on, and I remember being curled up on the couch just like when I was a child. My mind was racing. What is this? I thought. Why is he so angry? Why is he yelling and throwing things at me? It's not like I wanted it to happen. Who is he?

ABUSE

The car accident unleashed something in Petar. Something I'd never seen before. The way he threw things at me, yelled at me, and made me feel like an illiterate and incapable person just because of a minor car accident broke my heart. I got so stressed and anxious that I stopped driving. For six months, I would walk three miles a day to the bus station before standing on my feet all day at work, only because I was scared to drive. It was exhausting. I have never been skinnier.

On our first Orthodox Easter in the US, we were invited to a friend's house for lunch. It is a Bulgarian tradition to boil and color eggs on Easter, and as a surprise, I prepared an egg for every guest. There were to be only six of us. I stored the eggs in my black leather backpack. On our way to the party, we picked up some wine. I was excited to eat Easter lamb with a green salad and to instigate a traditional egg fight with the eggs I was bringing.

After we arrived, I immediately began to help prepare the table with the others. A moment later, I saw Petar digging around inside my backpack. By now, I knew how he wanted to control and know everything, and I worried about the eggs.

"What are you looking for?" I asked.

He didn't answer, so I approached him and repeated my question. Unexpectedly, he stood up and slapped me in the face. I didn't know what to do. Embarrassed because our friends saw what he had done to me, I longed for the earth to open up and swallow me. In shock, I went to one of the bedrooms to hide and cry. The only question on my mind was: Why? I knew by then that Petar had anger issues, but still! I hadn't done anything. Everyone acted as if nothing had happened when I emerged from the room.

On the way back home, I remembered the promise I'd made to myself: *Never to tolerate physical abuse from anyone.* When I reached our apartment, I told Petar that if he ever hit me again, I would call the police. I mentioned that this was not Bulgaria, where such behavior was "acceptable."

"Luckily, we live in the United States," I said, "where I have rights, and you can go to jail for violating them."

He never hit me again, but he became increasingly emotionally, verbally, and financially abusive.

When upset, he would yell at me, kick walls and doors, and throw objects at me. He forbade me to see people he thought were "not good" for me. He told me what I could and couldn't wear and what I should and shouldn't eat or do. He even forbade me from eating chocolate, as he said: "You tend to get fat, and you will become a very soft jelly-like fat woman with lots of cellulite all over your body." He controlled our money and expenses and insisted on approving everything I wanted to buy. He often made me return things because they were "too expensive," even when they were not.

We fought all the time. I begged him to change. Many times, I told him that if he continued his behavior, I would file for a divorce. I'll never forget his answer:

"You wouldn't survive a day alone in this country."

"You are nothing without me!"

DIVORCE

A year and a half after we got married, I decided to find a better-paying job so that I could support myself and file for a divorce. I couldn't take it anymore.

To avoid making Petar angry and aggressive, I waited until he was on a trip to Bulgaria. Then, I moved out of the apartment and rented another one with a roommate. Finally, I filed for a divorce. We hadn't even been married for two years.

I was brought up in a country where divorce was perceived as a failure and something that only losers do. I had to overcome the fact that I would become one of those people and admit I had failed.

Telling my family back home was not easy. My mother couldn't believe her favorite son-in-law would treat me like that. Surprisingly, she took my side and supported me during the process. My father didn't say anything. He acted as if nothing happened.

Petar didn't want to divorce me. I was just one of his possessions he didn't want to let go of. He found out where I lived and came by a few times with flowers and presents. He called me all the time to say he was sorry and told me he would change. I was firm. I didn't see any potential for change. And how could I forgive him for all the abuse and humiliation?

When he saw that he wouldn't lure me back, he became angry and decided to make things difficult. First, he started threatening me that he would go to the immigration office and tell them I only married him for the green card. Then, realizing he had no case, he refused to sign the legal divorce agreement that stated neither of us wanted anything from the other. I tried to make it as easy as possible and even left him all of the household items and the second car (which I was paying for), but he still didn't accept the divorce. He was on a mission. a mission to make me miserable.

After a while, I had no other choice. I told him that if he refused to proceed with the divorce in Bulgaria, I would start one in the United States, where I wouldn't be the only one paying for all the legal lawyer fees. I would take my car, possessions, and money back. That got him. Material possessions were always crucial to him. Stingy and fearful of losing out, he finally agreed to sign. It took a lot longer than a simple divorce should have, but after nine months, it was finalized.

ALONE

After the divorce, I was lonely and sad and suffered severe anxiety attacks.

It was excruciating to see my friends taking a side and turning their backs on me. But eventually, I decided that if they reacted like that, then they were probably not really my friends to begin with.

During those days, there was no Skype, Viber, FaceTime, or any of the free communication applications we have today. Using a prepaid calling card, I could only afford to call my family or friends in Bulgaria once a week.

The only comfortable place outside of the shared two-bedroom apartment was my work. Luckily, it was only a five-minute drive from home. I remember going there to escape the loneliness, but I still had a difficult time with anxiety. To manage the attacks, I would go home during my lunch break to take a cold shower to get through the rest of the day. It was tough. Sometimes, I was taking three to four cold showers a day.

Then, one Sunday, I noticed a rash. It covered my body. I freaked out. I thought it might be chicken pox. Immediately, I went to the emergency room to see a doctor. Sitting and waiting my turn,

I thought, *"What if it's contagious, and I must stay home? My roommate is on vacation, and I have no one to call to bring me food or anything else I might need."* I even started wondering if I should go back to Bulgaria. That was always an option, right? But then I thought: this would be my ex-husband's victory. He wanted to isolate me, and he was succeeding. If I went back, it would prove his words:

"You wouldn't survive a day alone in this country. You are nothing without me." I couldn't allow it. I might be alone, sick, and miserable, but I won't quit. I'll survive.

When it was my turn to see the doctor, he performed a routine exam and told me it was a virus. It seemed strange for a virus to cause a rash, but I went to the drugstore and bought the medicine he prescribed. For a week, I was at home alone.

I was alone, but I was free.

MARIJUANA

Back in the days of communist Bulgaria, there was not an illicit drug problem in the country. We were told that drugs were only available in capitalist countries, and that was why they had poor and homeless people, and we didn't. Alcohol was another story. It was technically not allowed until a person reached eighteen, but no one was strict about it. Underaged children were often buying alcohol and cigarettes for their parents, and the stores were allowed to sell them to them.

After a few years of living in the United States, I realized that pretty much everyone had smoked marijuana at least once. When a friend found out I never had, she gave me some for my thirtieth birthday.

It was late at night in the middle of the week when I decided to try it. I'd already had two scotches and four or five cigarettes. My boyfriend Mitko, and I went outside. I inhaled once and held the smoke in my lungs. I repeated this a few more times, and pretty soon, I started laughing. I have never laughed so uncontrollably in my whole life. Mitko was laughing, too. Everything was funny. So funny that tears were falling from my eyes.

Then something changed. I suddenly felt hot. So hot that I had to take off my clothes and lay down naked on the wooden floor.

I thought my heart would explode. I asked my boyfriend to bring me some ice. He filled up a big zip-lock bag and put it on my chest. I started to feel a little better but kept thinking that I would probably die. I even considered calling 911 for help, but I got scared since marijuana was illegal in California back then.

After laying there, who knows for how long, the terrible heat turned freezing cold. Mitko helped me get up and make my way to the couch, and I asked him to bring me all the blankets in the house. I felt like I was naked in the middle of the North Pole. Shaking violently, I didn't know what to think or do. After maybe half an hour, I got hot again, and I had to lay back down on the hardwood floor with the ice pack on my chest. These hot and cold episodes continued all night long.

In the morning, I was so exhausted I threw up, which immediately made me feel a little better. I desperately wanted to call in sick to work, but I knew my boss would be very unhappy about it and make my life miserable the next day.

I promised myself that I would never take any drugs ever again.

ENOUGH

One of the mutual friends I shared with my ex-husband was my immediate supervisor at the company where I worked. She was the Controller, and I was the Staff Accountant. After the divorce, she had said to me, "I admire your bravery," but shortly thereafter, she turned against me. Under his influence, she decided that it was wrong that I had left him, and she took his side. I guess she adopted his agenda: *to make my life miserable.*

At work, she gave me impossible tasks, took credit for things I completed, and started closing her office door so that I would feel more and more isolated in my little cubicle in front of her glass wall. Eventually, it became too much for me. I got sick.

Every morning before I went to work, I suffered severe stomach pains. Then I started throwing up. Even though I didn't eat breakfast, I would still throw up stomach juices. At one point, everything became so severe that I could barely walk upright.

My doctor told me, "You are probably too young for this, but it might be stomach cancer."

I was only thirty years old. He said he needed to run some tests, an x-ray, and a colonoscopy. I freaked out.

After all those medical interventions on my body, the results came back negative. My doctor said he saw nothing abnormal, so that might be stress.

A few months later, I asked to take a vacation to visit my newborn nephew in Bulgaria. My boss said she couldn't give me that time off, and after a friendly lunch with the company's chief financial officer, she refused to sign my vacation request. Both of them told me that if I wanted to go and see my nephew, I would have to quit. As miserable as I was with that job, I decided it might be a good idea.

After my resignation, I filed for unemployment. After all, they made me quit, and I had a legal right to collect unemployment after two and a half years of working there. The unemployment department had to contact my ex-employer to ensure my statements were truthful. When they talked with my ex-boss, she told them they didn't force me to quit and that I did it just because I wanted to. My case was rejected.

Then, for the first time in my life, I decided to fight back. What they said was not right, and I would prove it. I filed for an appeal. They set a date and time when both sides would meet before a judge.

When the day came, that familiar pain in my stomach also returned. *Did I deserve to get sick over this?* I was so stressed that I remember very little, but one thing I remember clearly—the judge asked my ex-boss: "If you say she was a good worker and very valuable to the company, why didn't you approve her three weeks' vacation request?" I don't remember her answer, but a week later, I received a letter stating that my appeal was accepted and my unemployment was granted.

Finally, I thought, there is justice.

After that, I stopped throwing up every morning and taking cold showers.

TRAPPED

As time passed, I started wondering what to do with my life. I'd always loved painting, and now that no one could stop me, I began to paint as a hobby. It was a profoundly healing and therapeutic experience. My boyfriend, Mitko, was supportive and encouraged me in anything I wanted to do—something I'd never experienced before. I gave paintings as gifts to friends and my sister, and everyone loved them. I found it interesting, but not at all surprising, that my parents never commented on my paintings. It was like they couldn't see them hanging on the walls.

As much as I enjoyed painting, I couldn't make a living from it. But I knew I didn't want to work as an accountant anymore, *so what then?* I'd always been drawn to design but thought I was too old for it.

Mitko suggested that I study Real Estate. He was passionate about it and felt I could be good at it. As I researched the best online schools, I discovered two types of licenses. One is a Real Estate Agent, and the other is a Real Estate Broker. At first, I thought I might study to become a real estate agent, but I realized that because of my financial background, it made more sense to study to become a real estate broker. The difference was that with the Broker License, I could have my own company, and people could work for me. It would not be easy, but I wanted more options at the end.

Again, I found myself studying something I wasn't passionate about. I had to read and memorize a lot of dry material, requirements, and laws. The prerequisite classes included Real Estate Practice and Principals, Finance, Appraisal, and Economics and Property Management. I passed all of them on my first try but didn't find any joy in it. Next, I would apply for a license at the California Department of Real Estate, and in 2004, one year after quitting my accounting job, I became a licensed Real Estate Broker.

Finding an office to work in was easy. The hours were flexible, and I got to be my own boss. *This was precisely what I wanted, so why was I still unhappy?*

It didn't take long for me to realize that I didn't want to do Real Estate. Some people enjoy sales, but I'm not one of them. I decided to switch to another part of Real Estate: Property Management. Before opening a company, I thought working for someone else would be a good idea to ensure I enjoyed it.

I did not. Property management was a job that required taking tons of phone calls daily, during which tenants would complain about things not working or other negative situations.

At this point, I didn't know what to do, so I switched back to accounting.

You would think that I would learn, but no. Again, trapped in my old ways, I had invested immeasurable time and energy for someone else. I learned a lot that would help me later in my life, but the biggest lesson was facing the reality of diving into something I didn't enjoy without first questioning myself.

Was it my second nature to always do what people close to me told me to?

YOGA

When I began to practice yoga, it was a coincidence, even though I don't really believe in coincidence.

The first class I attended was packed. I remember thinking: "What am I doing here? I'm not skinny and flexible." Nervous, I found a little spot for my mat and waited. The teacher opened the class with a seated meditation. I found it challenging to sit with closed eyes and avoid looking at the people around me. Next, we were given instructions with the names of the poses that I knew nothing about. I could only try my best to copy what everyone else was doing.

When the class ended, we were given a final meditation in which I had to put the palms of my hands together in front of my heart—an action so foreign to me that at first, I resisted, but when the teacher explained that it was a way of connecting with our hearts and that it would change the way we feel, I decided to overcome the discomfort and try it. I found myself overcome with peace.

I decided to continue with the classes, and after a while, I even started to enjoy them. The part I liked the most was the teacher's pattern. He was constantly talking, and from this, I learned many interesting and outside-the-box things. I became interested in yogic philosophy, nutrition, healing arts, and qi gong—including medical qi gong. I bought many books and started educating myself on each subject.

After a few years of practice, I began attending workshops. I will never forget the one called: *"Feeding Your Demons."* Honestly, I signed up out of sheer curiosity. There, I found myself surrounded by only yoga teachers, and when the facilitator asked me why I had come, I replied that I liked her picture on the flyer.

The workshop started with instructions to close our eyes and keep them closed until the end of the process. Then, we had to take nine deep relaxation breaths. With the first three breaths, we had to release our physical tension, followed by our emotional tension, and finally, our mental tension. Afterward, we had to create a heartfelt motivation to dedicate that practice to our benefit and for the benefit of all beings. Then, the real work began.

The first step was to find the demon in the body. We were asked to scan our bodies and try to locate where the demon was abiding. To my surprise, my demon was located in my uterus. Then, we had to identify its shape, color, texture, and temperature. To my even bigger surprise, I found out that my demon had a sticky texture; it was black and burning hot.

We were told to allow this sensation, color, texture, and temperature to intensify and then move out of our bodies and become personified in front of us. To my astonishment, my opposite was a handsome young boy, sitting cross-legged, lean but muscular, much taller than me, with shiny black hair, silky milk chocolate skin, and penetrating green eyes that radiated anger.

Suddenly, I realized that this was my son—the one I was supposed to have but chose not to. Shocked by the comprehension, I continued to listen to the facilitator's guidance. She told us that when we really feel connected with the ally's energy, we need to ask four questions: How will you help me? How will you protect me? What pledge do you make to me? And how can I access you?

Then, we had to physically change places and become the ally, settle into its body, look at ourselves from its point of view, and answer the questions.

From the perspective of my unborn child, I saw myself very differently and was able to answer all of the questions.

Only after allowing my unborn child's eyes to penetrate my body was I able to feel all the love he held for me. He was not angry at me anymore. He was joyful, loving, and pleased that I could do what I wanted. Then, I watched him dissolve into a golden mist. This I could feel all over my body, integrating into every cell. At last, I dissolved, too. There was no more feeling of the body.

After that experience, I stopped feeling guilty that I decided not to have any children, and I became more connected with myself and with the invisible world.

HEAVEN

One day, my mother complained about my father to me over the phone. I said she should have done something about it if she'd been so unhappy all these years.

"I stayed because of you," she said. "If it weren't for you and your sister and the problems you gave me, things would have been different."

I tried to stay calm, mentioning that I hadn't lived with them for the past twenty years and she could have made changes since then. Then she told me I needed to think about what I'd done to her—by which she meant my first boyfriend and the divorce, and the implication that all of her health problems were because of me.

"I don't know what happiness is for you," she said, "but this is life, and things are the way they are."

When I hung up, I started to cry. All of my life, I'd struggled with the fact that my parents ignored me and I was nothing to them. It wasn't the first such conversation I've had with my mother, but this one, in particular, was a bit too much. All those feelings of not being wanted, loved, or understood rushed back in. I grew angry. I was angry about the way I was treated and how I was always the one to take the blame. No matter what I tried to do to please them, it was never enough.

Desperate to get this anger out of my system, I started cleaning. I scrubbed everything in the house that needed scrubbing up to the point where it hurt my right hand. Just when I couldn't move it anymore, I stopped. Then, I drank two glasses of wine and skipped lunch. This helped me to relax, but not nearly enough. I decided to go to the sauna and then to yoga.

The sauna was empty. I laid on my white towel and tried to calm down. Before closing my eyes, I looked at the wall clock in front of me—4:15 pm. Hugged in warmth, I felt better and more at peace.

I saw a road before me. Hundreds of people lined up on its left shoulder. All of them were clothed in white. They stood side by side, smiling at me, each present and loving. At the end of the road was nothing but a big, white circle of light. It felt very inviting, and I wanted to be there. Directly to my right was a woman. Her beautiful waist-long white hair hung freely, and her eyes beamed toward me with love, compassion, and understanding. Our eyes locked, and she touched my face. I have never before felt so much love and acceptance. It felt like she was my mother—the mother I always needed and wanted.

I was at home. I was in heaven.

All at once, I heard the other people telling me: "It's not your time," then echoing over and over: "Not your time, not your time." Several of them walked up to me and pushed me so hard that I started falling. It felt like I was falling off a cliff. I took a deep breath and almost jumped off the sauna bench where I was lying. I sat up and opened my eyes. The clock on the wall showed 5:15 pm. I immediately got out of there and lay down on one of the benches outside.

That evening in my bed, I realized that not only had I nearly died, but subconsciously, I'd tried to kill myself. I was very aware of what may happen if I drank wine instead of water (and on an empty stomach) before going into the sauna.

Why did I do it? I asked myself. Why can't I stop reacting in this way? Punishing myself whenever the people I love hurt me.

BRAVE

One morning, I woke up with a new idea. I wanted to combine a few images and create one using single elements from each one. I sat in front of my computer and tried to implement my idea. After a few hours of unsuccessful efforts, I gave up. Maybe I could find some courses to help me, I thought. I got into my car and headed down to the local college.

At the information center, I discovered the fall semester had already begun. I was two weeks late. The girl at the center saw my desperation and told me that I needed to talk to the Photoshop teacher if I wanted to sign up. He was in class at the moment, but I was welcome to wait until it finished. She explained that even though I was late, if there was an opening in the class, he could give me a unique number to sign up.

As I waited in front of the classroom's glass walls, I allowed my excitement to overcome my never-ending anxiety about talking to people I didn't know. By the time the class was over, I was ready. I introduced myself to the professor and told him how much I wanted to learn Photoshop. He said that his class was overbooked, but he knew of another class, focused more on digital photography, that might have some openings. It was disappointing but not the end of the world. At least I'd learn something.

He walked me to meet the other professor and listened as I explained what I wanted to accomplish. After I got my sign-in number for the digital photography class, the Photoshop professor said, "Come to my office. I'll give you a number, too."

I couldn't believe my luck. Maybe my enthusiasm won him over. I will take two classes that semester: Digital Photography and Level 1 Photoshop.

I was anxious telling Mitko about what had happened. I worried he might get angry because I hadn't asked him, but to my surprise, he was supportive. He said he was happy for me to learn something I was passionate about.

I could have guessed what my parents were going to say. My mother's immediate reaction was: "Studying at 38 years old? Oh my god, dear, you are making me laugh. After you graduated from the University, didn't you say you would never study anything ever again?"

"But this is different," I said. "This is something I'm passionate about."

She replied, "Well, I'm just reminding you of your words. That's all."

My father's response was, "Work is not something you should enjoy. Hobbies are for things you like to do."

It was a depressing conversation. *When would I stop looking for their approval?*

Later, my passion for photography and creativity would expand into more classes. After two and a half years, I completed the Graphic Design program with straight A's.

PARADISE

Mitko and I lived together for almost a decade. Like in every relationship, we had our ups and downs, but overall, we were very compatible and able to accomplish anything we put our minds to. Everyone kept asking us why we weren't getting married, but we always said we didn't see the point.

One morning, Mitko called me excitedly and told me to meet him at my favorite French restaurant. When I arrived, I found him very nervous. He was holding a small bag. Once seated at the table, he began telling me things like, "This is long overdue," and "You mean so much to me." From the bag, he withdrew a small box. I felt my blood rushing through my body.

He pushed the little gold-like button in front of the box, and the lid opened. Inside was a classic, clean, brilliant-cut design diamond ring with a platinum band. I loved it.

After eleven years of living together, my boyfriend proposed. With tears in my eyes, I said, "Yes."

Five months later, I was sitting in the front seat of the Wrangler Jeep that was taking me to my favorite beach of Ke'e, on the garden island of Kauai. As a teenager, I had watched Meggie Cleary & Ralph de Bricassart in the classic TV series *"The Thorn Birds."* I vividly recalled the scene where he came to her while she was standing with her feet in the ocean, looking at the horizon. To me, that beach was the most picturesque place on earth. The backdrop of the mesmerizing Na'Pali coast and its lush tropical greenery made it unforgettable. Having our wedding there was a dream come true.

The ceremony only included the government officiator, the photographer, and a friend of ours. The photographer and our friend served as witnesses. Mitko wore a stylish tuxedo, and I wore a mid-length, light pink silk dress. We stood in a circle of white and pink Plumeria flowers. The weather was sunny, but not too hot. It was an hour before sunset.

As we exchanged our vows, the weather changed. The clear and sunny sky became cloudy and windy. When we put our wedding rings on each other, a tropical storm had arrived and started to rain. Having come from a very suspicious culture, I couldn't help thinking. What does this mean? *Will this marriage be like hell again?* The weather had been weird during my first wedding, and that didn't finish well.

Reading my mind, the official told me that the Hawaiians believe such things are a good omen. I didn't trust her. But then, suddenly, the sky cleared, and the setting sun returned just in time to go down. The photographer took several pictures of us, the background, and the sunset.

On the way back in the car, I kept hoping we'd made the right decision. There was that uneasy feeling in my stomach again, and it was not going away. I wondered if it was because of the weather or if there was something else...

BETRAYAL

Shortly after my wedding, I went to Bulgaria to visit my family. Mitko followed two weeks later so that we could get together and celebrate with my parents, my sister, and her family. But when he arrived, I found him to be different. He was constantly doing things on his phone and not really communicating much with either myself or anyone else. I figured he must have a lot of work, but that didn't explain my uneasy feeling.

When we returned to the US, I noticed him doing some laundry (which he never does). I found a strange Korean dessert in the freezer and discovered long black hairs everywhere throughout the house. When I asked him about the dessert, he told me he went to a Korean store to buy it because someone had recommended it. I knew he was lying.

From then on, his behavior grew increasingly unusual. He started working late, even on the weekends. He became very attached to his phone, up to the point where he didn't leave it behind, even when going to the bathroom. I tried to tell myself everything was okay, that it was all in my mind, and I gave my full attention to my studies in college.

One night, my hubby didn't wake up when I got up from bed to go to the bathroom. I made a split decision to check out his phone. I knew his passcode and started looking through the messages, where I saw nothing suspicious. Then, I got creative. I figured deleted messages must be stored somewhere. After a long search, there it was. A folder of deleted items. And boom! There was a confirmation of my uneasy feeling, which had haunted me for over a few months.

Involuntarily, my whole body started to shake. It took a lot of will to calm down. I decided that instead of reading the messages, I should take pictures of them. Because he could wake up any moment, I needed to be as fast as possible. As I scrolled and snapped, I kept seeing words like love, girl, surprise, *and even Korea.* I felt like waking him up and confronting him right away, but something inside told me to wait, so I climbed back into bed.

Lying next to him, I looked out into the room's darkness. I couldn't sleep. Those became some of the most prolonged hours of my life. I started recalling over and over all of the little situations where he had been constantly with his phone, coming home late, working on the weekends, and treating me cold. Like little flashbacks, they were coming back at me one after another.

In the morning, after my spouse went to work, I sat in the office and started looking over my pictures of the messages. I learned that he was involved with a girl named Sunny, who apparently was from Korea. In the messages, they told each other how in love they were and how lucky they were to be together, making plans to see each other the next day. It turned out she was waiting for some news from her home. There was some money involved. I couldn't believe my eyes. But the last conversation made me freeze.

Sunny: "They ask me when marry?"

Mitko: "So?"

Sunny: "I'll tell them soon :-*"

Sunny: "I don't say date..."

Mitko: ":-)"

Sunny: "Hey... you still want?"

Mitko: "Sun... you are my only girl. I want to marry y"

Sunny: "Did you tell her you and me very serious?"

Mitko: "Yes."

Sunny: "She marry?"

Mitko: "Not yet".

I started to cry with intense pain. Putting the pieces together, I realized that not only was he cheating on me, but it had been going on for a while, for so long, that he had promised to marry this woman. On top of that, he told her that I was not with him anymore and that I was getting married to someone else soon. Wow! Really?

My mind was racing like a crazy horse and couldn't stop. I had a difficult time processing and believing what I saw. What is going on? Why was money involved? Why had he married me just four months ago?

CONFRONTATION

After processing the fact that I had been betrayed in the most awful way I could imagine, I decided to confront him and find out what was going on.

The next day, I skipped one of my evening classes at the college and told Mitko to come home early because I wanted to talk to him. He resisted at first but ultimately agreed. I had some appetizers ready for him, and we sat together in the family room. He was nervous, and so was I.

Being direct by nature, I asked: "Are you seeing someone else?"

Right away, he became defensive and said: "No! Why do you think that?"

"I won't be mad," I told him calmly. "Just tell me the truth because I hate when people lie to me, especially those closest to me."

I could see him getting agitated. "What are you talking about?" he said. "I'm just very busy with work."

I asked him to give me his phone. He hesitated, but he did. I went to the deleted history and showed him all the text messages he thought he'd gotten rid of. He was stunned. For a minute, he didn't know what to say. The silence was heavy.

Finally, he started talking. He admitted that he was having an affair, but there was more. He told me that before we got married, he wanted to experience sex with an Asian woman. His friend told him about a brothel and that it was great because there were no attachments. He said he went there a couple of times and fell for a particular Korean girl who called herself Sunny. She told him she was working as a prostitute to support her father, who needed to have a cancer operation. Unfortunately, this was just the beginning.

Mitko had decided to help her not only so that she could stop working as a prostitute, but so her father could get his operation. Apparently, he was paying for her apartment and expenses and had given her an extensive check for her father's treatment. Being good with finances and money management, I couldn't believe the amount of money he had given her, but that was the least of my problems at that time. After some time, he started to feel she was using him for money. He tried to stop the madness, but then something else happened. He started receiving threats from some Korean people who knew Sunny. They told him that if he stopped paying her, they would come and tell me what was going on, or worse, do something bad to me, so he continued to pay.

I did not want to believe what I was hearing. It felt like I was in a mafia movie. All of the essential ingredients were there: money, prostitution, threats of violence, and innocent people.

"What are you going to do?" I asked.

He tried to assure me that everything was already under control and that he was planning to stop seeing her. I didn't believe him.

After a few more questions and answers, I felt drained. I went to bed in a state of emotional exhaustion with a massive headache, hoping that somehow the next day would fix everything.

DEPRESSION

The next morning, the feelings that haunted me all of my life came back again. If no one wants me and loves me, why am I living? Curled on the kitchen bench, all I could think about was how much I hated my lonely, miserable life. My head felt heavy and tense, like a mountain volcano that would erupt at any moment. The loudest question was: How should I end this misery once and for all? I'm tired of trying and failing. I'm tired of being alive.

For as long as I can remember, I tried to be a good person, a good daughter, student, and wife. Where had I gone wrong? My parents were never happy with me. My teachers were harsh to me. My partners didn't appreciate me. What did I do to deserve it?

The feeling of not being worthy. The feeling of being rejected, betrayed, and humiliated. What was worse than that? This was it for me. I couldn't take it anymore. The only thing I could think of was: How should I kill myself?

Being unsuccessful with cuts and pills this time, I decided to kill myself by hanging. I came up with two options: either hang myself in the garage because the ceiling was higher and it had conveniently exposed strong beams, or use the olive tree in the back yard because it was the strongest and biggest tree and it wouldn't break from my weight.

Then, other thoughts started creeping in. What if I am unsuccessful like before? What will happen to Mitko? I know he hurt me, but does that mean that I have to hurt him back? I knew he would be devastated. I couldn't imagine him coming home and seeing me hanging dead on a rope. He couldn't take that. He would probably kill himself, too, or become an alcoholic or a drug addict. I didn't want that for him.

Then what? I thought. Maybe I should start praying. Being brought up during the communist regime, I grew up without religion. To me, words like God and Jesus were very foreign. I never read the Bible or any other religious texts, but I believed in spirits. I always thought that there was something out there. Something not as remote as God but a kind of ever-present spirit or energy.

In an act of desperation, I started to pray. Almost every night, after fighting and then drinking a bottle of wine or who knows how many shots of vodka, I would go to bed and cry. While crying, I silently prayed. *I prayed to die.*

I prayed to all that might be out there—the gods, spirits, energies, angels, and demons. I didn't leave anyone out. I said: *"Please, god, angels, demons, spirits, and guides. Please let me die tonight. Please let me die in my sleep. I want to die from a heart attack or something that would take me right away. If that is not possible, please let me have some accident and die without hurting other people. Please let me die. Please! Please! Please! I don't want to live. I don't want to be here. What am I doing on this Earth? Why do I have to go through all of this? Please let me die."*

Eventually, after praying and crying until I was exhausted, I would fall asleep for a couple of hours.

And in the morning, my first thought was always: Why am I still alive? I've heard that people get what they want when they pray hard enough. Why was I still here? Now, I have to get through another day.

One morning, mad because of the fact I didn't die, I got into my car and went to the store. I parked my car in the parking lot and went inside. Standing in front of the rope and chain section, I tried to decide on the best one for my purpose. There were so many choices between textures and sizes. Which one is the best for hanging? Then a salesperson came in and asked me:

"Are you looking for a rope or a chain?"

With a soft voice, I answered: "A rope?"

Then he said: "What do you need it for?"

Speechless, I felt my face turn red, and I couldn't look at the person's eyes. I didn't expect that question. To get out of the situation, I mumbled: "For a home project," and for him to leave me alone, I added, "I will let you know once I decide." A few minutes after he left, I walked out of the store embarrassed and empty-handed.

RAGE

The months following my discovery of Mitko's betrayal were difficult. We had never fought before. During the twelve years of living together, we managed to resolve problems without drama. But now all that has changed. We started fighting.

The only positives in my life were going to college and working on the assigned projects. Nothing else could help me get my mind off what happened or ease the tension of how I had somehow found myself in a similar situation to my first marriage. Of course, the details were different, but interestingly, both marriages began in May, and in both, the fighting started in September.

While doing my best to wrap my mind around the events, I continued to find messages between him and her, and the fights became more prolonged and more emotional. I was upset he didn't see that this woman was just using him. She was clearly a very good manipulator, and it was likely that her friends were still threatening him. He wasn't telling me everything.

One morning, after fighting all night, I decided I'd had enough. I removed all my clothes from the closet and placed them on the bed. Halfway through the process, something stopped me. I sat on the bed among the clothes and started crying. I cried and cried for hours. I thought, "I can't just leave him in this situation. She will take everything he owns. He doesn't have anyone else to help him." I loved and cared about Mitko too much to leave and watch him being destroyed. I knew I was stronger and that I could help him get through this situation. I also knew that it would be at my expense, but I decided to do it anyway.

The months passed by. Sometimes he was seeing her, and sometimes he wasn't. Night after night, I found my anger increasing at him for dragging it out for so long, at myself for staying with him, and at the Universe for putting me through this.

One late night, after he lied to me again, I got so upset that I took all the pictures from our wedding album and started tearing them apart. I didn't just tear them in half. I tore the halves in half and so on until the pieces were so small that they were unrecognizable. I was in the zone—the zone of rage.

He couldn't believe it. Crying himself, he tried to stop me, but I was unstoppable. Desperate and sobbing, I screamed at him: "How could you do this to me? How could you cheat on me before, during, and after our wedding? What kind of a person does that?"

I was going through constant and enormous emotional pain. The fights got so out of control that I wanted to destroy every object in the house. There were a few nights when I slept in my car. I had no place else to go because it was too embarrassing for me to admit to any of my friends what was going on and that my second marriage was turning out worse than the first. Meanwhile, my rage and despair were building up. I thought I was going crazy.

AGAIN

One year after everything began, things finally calmed down. We weren't fighting as much, and it looked like he had finally stopped seeing her. I was going through my last semester at college, and for a change, I didn't have to put on tons of make-up to cover up my puffy-from-crying-and-sleep-deprived eyes.

Seven months later, when everything in our relationship was moving towards healing, I once again heard that voice in my head telling me to check his phone. I stopped doing that some time ago, but now I have decided to listen to my intuition. I looked at the messages, deleted messages, and apps, and I found something strange. There was an app that I didn't recognize. It was called *"Kakao Talk"* and apparently was from Korea. His account had only one contact. I looked at the contact's pictures and saw an Asian girl in her bathing suit by the swimming pool, along with a selfie in her car. I thought, "Again? But why does this one look different?" I couldn't be sure, but it appeared to be another girl. What surprised me most was how unsurprising it was and how it didn't really hurt anymore.

Over the next few weeks, I checked his phone every chance I had, but there were never any messages in the app. Then, one day, while he was outside trimming the avocado tree in our backyard without his phone, I checked again, and there it was. Messages between him and that nameless Asian girl. Her account only showed a dot, so I called her the *Dot Girl*. From these few texts he forgot to delete, I found out they were seeing each other. It was a brand-new affair.

I had told him last time that if he ever did this again, I would file for a divorce, but how could I file for a second divorce in the second year of my second marriage? I was desperate to understand why the things were repeating again.

My body was in pain, my mind was confused, and my soul was in sorrow. What had I done to deserve this? It was difficult for me to admit that I had tried and failed again. It was even more challenging to tell my friends or family. What would they think of me? I heard my mother's voice in my head, saying repeatedly: "What will people say? Second divorce!?"

I didn't understand why he was doing this. I felt sad, lost, embarrassed, and humiliated. But most of all, I felt unwanted. All of my life, I'd suffered from the fact that no one wanted me. My mother obviously didn't want me. My father would rather have had a boy. My ex-husband abused me, and my new one was cheating on me. What was wrong with me?

I tried so hard to please everyone I loved and cared about, but I could never get what I craved.

After fighting with myself and overcoming the fact that this was another mistake in a fucked-up life full of mistakes, I filed for divorce.

BROKE

After filing the paperwork, I came home and told Mitko. He burst into tears and pleaded with me. "No, please, no. I'm sorry. I'm so sorry that I did it again. I just got caught up and didn't know what to do."

"I told you," I said, "that if I ever found out you were doing it again, that would be the end. Why didn't you believe me? Why does no one believe me anyway?"

After the initial shock, we started communicating. We were both in pain. I explained the divorce paperwork and showed him how much he needed to pay me.

"But I can't afford it," he said.

"You are lying to me again," I replied. "I know how much you make, and this is fair for both of us."

Then he explained that he (or should I say we) didn't have any saved money. Not only that, but he was in debt, had taken out a loan from his pension fund, and even borrowed money from friends.

"But why did you do that?" I asked. "What happened?"

He said that he'd paid hundreds and thousands of dollars to the girl from his first affair. She really had manipulated him by telling him that it was for her and her sick father. After he realized the lie, he stopped paying, but then he started getting mafia-like threats from her *"friends."* He said that at one point, a gun was held to his head. I got chills when he told me this, but I didn't believe it. After so many lies, I thought this was another one to make me stay.

Mitko had always been good with money. He knew how to invest and manage money well. I wanted to see proof. I asked him to show me all of his accounts. He gave me access to everything, and I started auditing. After all, I had a masters in it. His bank account, retirement, and investment fund statements were a mess. As I gazed at the white-background web statements and their black numbers, I thought this must be some sort of a joke. He was broke. We were broke. The only positive was that he hadn't taken a home equity line of credit against the house.

We couldn't even afford a divorce. It was just impossible. He would have to catch up and return huge amounts of money not only to the credit cards and the retirement funds but also to his friends. It was unbelievable.

Broke, both financially and emotionally, *what could I do?* I'd just finished my graphic design program and was still looking for a job. I had no money to move out and rent a place alone.

My only option was to return to Bulgaria, which was no option. I endured all that hell just to run away back home. That would be the ultimate failure, and I would hate myself for the rest of my life. It wasn't that the situation there was so bad overall, but I'd always felt like an outsider, not only in my country of birth but even amongst my own family.

I was exhausted. It has been way too long, too painful, and too draining. I just wanted to go and live in a mountain cave. I didn't want to see anyone or deal with anything.

I withdrew the divorce application.

PART THREE

THERAPY

For many years, I kept telling Mitko that he needed to go to therapy to resolve some of his childhood issues. His answer was that he didn't believe in therapy. After he saw how serious I was about the divorce, he proactively sought out a therapist. First, he had a session alone; then, the therapist suggested we start going together. I agreed. I thought it would benefit us to understand what happened and why.

Spending every Saturday morning emotionally revisiting the events and reliving the situations was excruciating for me. Very often, I cried in the car on the way back home. It was difficult for both of us. The therapist kept saying: "All I hear is that you guys care about each other a lot." I knew this was true, but it took someone else noticing to make me realize it consciously.

Besides going to conventional therapy with Mitko, I went to unconventional treatment on my own. I wanted to discover what was wrong with me. Why did I always feel like life was torture? I had never understood people who said: "Life is so beautiful. It is the only one we have, so enjoy it." To me, life was never beautiful. I enjoyed only a few moments here and there, and I didn't think it was the only one I had.

A friend of mine recommended a guy named John the White Wolf. He had a psychology degree and worked at a college, but he also held a small private practice with alternative therapy group classes in the evenings. People called him a *"shaman"* because of his psychic abilities.

John was Japanese and about five and a half feet tall. He was about my age or younger, and in his naturally black hair, asymmetrically cut, wild, and straight, he wore a single white feather. During our first session in his cozy office, I discovered that our group was just him, one other lady, and me.

Thank god that it's just the three of us, I thought. Fewer people, less embarrassment, and less shame.

He started with a simple question, which didn't seem at all that simple at the time: Why are you here?

My face turned red. Then, in a soft and quiet voice, I said: "Because my husband cheated on me. Twice."

Then John asked me to elaborate, and over the next hour, I shared a condensed version of the story.

The other lady said: "Once, shame on you; twice, shame on me."

During another session a few weeks later, John said: "Your mother is a narcissist."

I wasn't exactly sure what a narcissist was. I knew that many of the significant rulers and dictators of the world were called narcissists, *but my mother?*

"Have you read *"Trapped in the Mirror?"*

"No," I replied.

"You should buy it," he said. "It would help you."

In my car, on the way back home, I couldn't stop wondering: What is a narcissist?

SICKNESS

After reading *"Trapped in the Mirror"* by Dr. Elan Golomb, I finally understood my mother's sickness. It was obvious in retrospect. *How had I not seen it sooner?* It had taken me until I was forty years old to realize that my mother was a narcissist.

The first thing I found out about narcissists is that they lack empathy. They think they are exceptional and entitled to everything. They seek validation and need to be looked upon with admiration, envy, and respect.

Narcissists can't control their emotions very well. This is why they will tend to fly off the handle. They can go into a rage at disappointments or frustrations and if things don't go their way.

Narcissistic parents are neglectful and selfish. They are unavailable and rarely present. They want their kids to be great achievers and good-looking and to serve as an example for others.

It was shocking and sad to recognize the destructive legacy narcissists leave for their children.

When I started connecting the dots, I realized that neither my mother nor my father were available for me. My mother was selfish. My father never showed emotion. They were never empathic and always wanted me to look good and be a good achiever. I had to be a straight-A student and an example for others. The question: *What will people say?* was always more important than my feelings.

I continued to read more books and watch videos on the subject. I learned that when a child gets abandoned, its brain gets programmed with rejection. It develops anxiety, detachment, psychological stress, and depression. Basically, the sense that life is not worth living.

I found out that no one can please a narcissist. That's why I was always unsuccessful in trying to please my mother. Because of that failure, I developed a high tolerance for mistreatment, and as a result, I did not maintain healthy boundaries with people I loved. All of this led me to decisions that would hurt me tremendously.

Because my parents devalued my emotions, I grew up with the feeling that I was not enough. I was not good enough as a daughter, as a partner, as a wife, or as a friend. As a result, I overcompensated.

I worked too much, and I did more than I should in every possible way. When that didn't work out, I grew angry with myself, and as a result, I hurt myself.

It became apparent that many of the things that happened in my life were the result of my coping mechanism brought on by the lack of love and attention I craved. I had become hypersensitive, and instead of becoming a narcissist myself, I went into protection mode.

The only way I could survive was to build a CAGE. a cage to hide away from the cruel, cold world I was living in.

SEARCH

Therapy was essential for me to start identifying the roots of my problems, but this was just the beginning of my healing process.

Both the conventional and unconventional sessions were helpful in their own way. Their emphasis on different methods allowed me to see my patterns from different angles. The couple's therapy with Mitko was explicitly targeted at our relationship and the one with John the White Wolf empowered me to confront my childhood and upbringing.

The lack of proper sleep and nourishment during the drama between Mitko and myself took a physical toll. My digestive system was jeopardized. I tried multiple diets and cleanses, but nothing worked. A few of my friends recommended a life coach and alternative methods healer. Her name was Cathy, and when I checked her website, I found out that she studied with teachers from all over the world, mainly from Asia and South America. I emailed her to make an appointment. *What do I have to lose?* I thought. I could always walk away.

Cathy ran her practice from home, where she kept an office. I was nervous when I rang the bell. One more treatment, I thought. When she opened the door, I saw a tall, skinny Caucasian girl with long, curly black hair. She seemed older than me, but it may have been because of her height. Her eyes reminded me of my mother's—tiny and bright green.

Before we started, she gave me a ten-page questionnaire and left the room. I was shocked at how much information she wanted. There were questions about everything, not only physical but emotional too, such as, did something significant and emotionally traumatic happen to me recently? Have I ever been divorced, and many more?

I was still finishing my responses twenty minutes later when Cathy returned. Then she sat in a chair in front of me, and while going through my answers, she asked even more questions.

Ultimately, she looked at me and said: "Your diet isn't that bad, but let's make it better. In addition to your habit of not eating junk or packaged food, I want you to stop eating all sweets, including fruits and sweet vegetables—no bread, dairy, beans, potatoes, or starchy food. Basically, your diet should include lots of greens, quinoa, barley, fish and a little meat. If you want fruit, you can eat berries."

"Pretty strict," I said.

"Yes, but it's the only way we can work on your digestive problems. To help you stay on track, I recommend a diet journal to make notes of everything you eat."

I was not pleased to see the diet excluding even carrots, peppers, eggplants, and tomatoes, but at that point, I was ready to do anything if it would get me back to normal, even a diet journal.

One month later, I'd lost some weight but didn't have much improvement in my digestive system. Then, during one of our conversations, Cathy said: "Everything is emotional. What has happened in your life recently? From your answers, I see that you had one divorce, which is pretty dramatic, but is there anything else?"

At first, I hesitated, but then I decided to tell her what happened with Mitko.

Cathy listened with interest, and when I was finished, she said:

"I've heard many stories, but nothing as extreme as this."

Then she added: "Mitko's soul is enlightened. He threw himself into this dangerous affair so that you could also become enlightened."

She must be joking, I thought.

For one thing, the word enlightened was way too out there for me, and for another, what does it really mean? *Was she trying to say that he cheated on me for me?* I had a challenging time digesting that.

PROCREATION

One day, Cathy and I had an argument.

She asked: "Why don't you have any children? This is how you transfer karma and how your energy will continue to live. It's also your responsibility. Many souls are waiting to be reincarnated."

My blood rushed into my face, and my heart was racing, but I tried to hide it.

"But you don't have children either, do you?" I replied. "Why do you want me to have them?"

Upset, she said, "I do have a child."

"A stepchild," I said. "It's not your own. You came into his life when he was seven years old. He has a biological mother, too." I didn't want to say all of this, but she'd pushed me.

Then, with tears in my eyes and a trembling voice, I continued:

"I was miserable during my childhood and throughout most of my life. I couldn't imagine bringing anyone into this world. I don't want to be responsible for anyone else's suffering."

After a pause, I continued: "How irresponsible would it be for me to transfer my karma, like you said, into an innocent baby who has done nothing to deserve it? Also, I keep hearing in the spiritual community that before a child gets born, its soul chooses its parents. Don't they say that to find an excuse for the mistreatment we grew up with?"

The walls closed in, and the room grew quiet. After an awkward silence, I continued: "Tell me. Why do you think my parents did all those things to me?"

With a dry voice, she replied: "Because they didn't know any better," "It's how they were treated as children, and that's why they treated you that way. It was just familiar and normal to them."

"We don't know that for sure," I replied.

"Your parents gave you life," Cathy insisted. "They built a roof over your head and provided food and clothes for you. That's enough! You should be grateful."

"Obviously, we disagree, and maybe we should stop the argument here," I said.

At home, I kept thinking about it. Ever since I got married for the first time, my family and friends have been putting pressure on me to have children. They told me it was my duty and the one way to find pure love.

I always thought that creating life should be taken seriously. It's a huge responsibility, and people should be ready for it.

WRITING

Attending therapy with Mitko, going to White Wolf alternative therapy, and Cathy's coaching led to a lot of intervention and self-reflection. I could barely digest it all. It helped me to recognize the conditioning of my upbringing and to analyze and understand the choices I made in life. That was all good and necessary, *but how could I break out?* Even though I could see a new and different world out there, how could I be a part of it? Recognition alone didn't mean I would have the guts to participate.

One evening during our group meetings, the White Wolf said: "Throughout your life, you haven't been yourself. You just adapted to different people and circumstances and took on the roles they expected from you. But that's not who you are."

Then he continued: "You had to hide yourself to survive. You had no other choice. You were never loved the way you wanted and needed to be."

Back home, I kept thinking... *If I wasn't myself, who was I?*

Angry at my life and the choices I'd made, I didn't know what to do. I didn't know where to hide. If I could erase everything from my mind, I would, but that was not possible. *What can I do now? Where should I begin?*

I decided that I needed an outlet, something more than photography, drawing, or painting. Those visual arts were not sufficient to express my feelings. a friend recommended *"The Artist's Way"* by Julia Cameron. She told me it was mainly for writers but also for other kind of artists.

"Follow the exercises," she said. "It will help you to find out what you want to do."

So I started writing. It was a strange experience since I'd never enjoyed writing before, *but had I known what I liked and didn't like?*

Manifesting my thoughts on paper felt liberating.

Writing brought me deeper into expressing my emotions. It helped me put things into perspective and see what happened and why. It assisted me in finding my inner voice. The one that was always there but never listened to.

In the process, I felt like I needed to go deeper. I needed to do something to help me open up to the world and show me that life is not only about suffering. Then, I remembered speaking with John about psychedelics. He'd told me how much they helped him during the dark days of his early twenties. I thought it was dangerous because my first and only experience with marijuana years before hadn't gone very well, but I was ready to try anything to get out of my cage. My depression still lingered. I needed resetting. The therapy was not enough.

INCEPTION

I put aside my fear and brought up to John my interest in alternative assisted healing with psychedelics. He recommended MDMA, explaining how it had proven therapeutic benefits, particularly among people with depression and other behavioral issues.

I was intrigued, so I engaged in online research to learn more. The articles I found explained how most users experienced feelings of empathy and oneness with the universe. After enough digging, I decided to try it. At that point, it felt like that was the only way to move forward.

I'd read that for the psychedelics to have a healing and therapeutic effect, supervision was advisable. I didn't want to risk wasting this opportunity, so I arranged a session with John the White Wolf. Before the session, we had a meeting where I explained the areas I wanted to focus on. Then, for my convenience, we agreed to do the session at my house.

The following week, we sat in my living room. He held space for me while I meditated on my intention. Then he gave me the pill and told me it would take about 45 minutes to an hour to start taking effect. Meanwhile, we talked a bit about my life and childhood.

"Borislava, you have the best poker face I have ever encountered. If I couldn't read energy, I would never be able to tell what you are going through right now."

"I worked on it my whole life," I said. "It is there to protect me. No one was allowed to see my true feelings."

An hour went by. Suddenly, my body started to feel like a cloud in the atmosphere. I was floating.

After a while, in suspension, I heard the White Wolf say: "Your poker face is gone now. How do you feel?"

"Awesome," I replied. "I have never felt better in my whole life."

Then he asked me to stand up. "Can you connect with the universe?" he said.

"Yes," I replied.

"See how high you can go without losing connection with your feet on the ground."

In my mind, it felt like my body had wings and flew up into space. I went pretty high, so high that at one point, I got scared. *What if I won't be able to return?* I thought.

"I'm very high," I said, "but I'm afraid to go any higher."

"It's okay. You don't have to. How do you feel?"

"I feel safe," I said. "It feels like a floating home base halfway to my real home."

"Good! Can you make yourself comfortable there?"

"Yes."

I sat on a white couch in my new home and observed the interior. Everything was white. The few furniture pieces, the rug, the frames on the wall, the lamps. As my mind's eye observed further, I noticed that it was built from a glass-like material, allowing me to see in all directions. There was nothing below my feet but a few little lights. Some of them were close, and some were far away.

"How do you feel in your new home?" He asked.

"I feel warmth and acceptance from the Universe."

"Very well," he said. "From now on, every time you feel depressed or suicidal, know that you can go to this place and find the love of the Universe. *From now on, you are not alone.*"

After the session, I went for a walk along a lake. I decided to sit on one of the benches to enjoy the view. Everything looked different somehow. I'd never before felt a part of this phenomenon called life. It was always like life and I were different entities. But sitting there, watching the sky, the clouds, the setting sun, the trees, the water, the birds, and other little animals and insects, I experienced a real connection for the first time. For the first time in my entire life, I felt calm, safe, and at peace.

POSSESSED

With all the changes in my emotional life, I wanted to enjoy more time outside. Curious to see the October 13th Harvest Full Moon, I drove out to Point Santa Cruz Lighthouse.

There, I found myself surrounded by a crowd of obnoxious, loud, drunk people. The air was thick with the various beats and clouds of smoke emanating from nearby cars. I decided to sit on a bench and wait for the moon. Before long, she emerged over the horizon: enormous, perfectly round, illuminating a brilliant, shining pathway on the Pacific Ocean.

I sat hypnotized by this vision for some time. Then, after a small glass of wine, I drove back to my house, only to find my body starting to tremble and my mind racing with weird thoughts as if it had been split into two.

What would happen if you jumped from the balcony? One side of my mind suggested.

It's the sixth floor, the other thought. *Why would I jump from a balcony anyway?*

Can you imagine what your body would look like on the concrete below? Or maybe you will survive, and this will be a way to experience the sensation of flight?

I don't want to feel that, I was thinking.

The conversation continued throughout the night. I was shaking the entire time, and I barely got any sleep. I don't remember how I survived until morning, but I felt a little relief when the sun came out.

Throughout the next day, my body continued to feel unsettled, and I couldn't do much of anything. I felt like there was an entity inside me who wanted to take over me. I didn't know what to do.

First, I called my mother. I told her that something was happening to me, that I didn't feel okay, that I felt possessed by something, and that I didn't know what to do. She suggested going to church to light a candle. I didn't see how this could help me. *I need something else.*

I called my sister and told her the same thing. She didn't have any ideas.

I texted the White Wolf, but he said he couldn't talk to me before Tuesday, two days away.

Then, in an act of desperation, I video-called Cathy.

"What can I do for you, Borislava," she asked coldly.

I explained that I had gone to the beach alone to look at the full moon surrounded by a drunken crowd. The moon had hypnotized me, I said, and I hadn't been myself since. I stretched out my hands and showed her how they were shaking, and I said that my whole body was shaking like that. She didn't seem to care much and said that no one could be possessed if they didn't allow it.

Mitko was on a business trip, and I didn't want to disturb him, but I called him next. He told me that I was powerful, that no entity could possess me, and that I knew what to do and how to care for myself. Then I realized that although I *did* know what to do, the shaking and all those crazy thoughts had prevented me from accessing my actual mind. I needed to take things one step at a time.

First, I put on 528 Hz high-frequency music. I had that playing day and night. Then, I lit some sage and cleaned myself and the apartment. I kept burning incencse all the time. Then, I scrubbed my shaking body with a mixture of ground coffee, sea salt, and coconut oil. I was already starting to feel much better.

But after a day or two, I still wasn't entirely back to myself, so I called White Wolf. He could tell at once that things weren't right.

When I explained the situation, he said: "It happened to you because you didn't believe it could. It happened to me too, years ago, because I didn't believe it could. Now you know it's possible, and if someone comes to you with that experience, you will understand them."

"But I'm not a healer," I said.

"Not yet." He replied.

SAMSARA

My relationship with Cathy continued to remain tense. With her help, I learned a lot about myself, but it was mainly through arguments. I often wondered why I kept going to see her when she irritated me so much.

One day, she told me, "Do you think it's easy dealing with your energy-grabbing energetic claws?"

I felt like she'd slapped me in the face. Probably, I would have preferred it. It wouldn't have been so painful.

"I hate your energy," she said. "It's very critical, and that's why Mitko cheated on you. Do you think it's easy being around you?"

I could barely hold my tears. How come even my coach didn't like me? What was I? A monster?

I cried in the car all the way home. Mitko asked me why I was so upset.

"Cathy told me that you cheated on me because my energy is very critical."

"That's not true," he said. "You are a very warm person. I cheated because I had my issues that had nothing to do with you. You are not critical. You are just honest, and I have always appreciated that quality in you."

After a little pause, he continued: "If she can't handle your honesty, maybe it will be good if you stop seeing her. At least for a while."

I nodded, but I wasn't sure what to do.

During the next few days, I was depressed and didn't feel like doing anything. My suicidal thoughts came back. I just wanted to die. Maybe my mother was right, I thought. Just like Cathy, she was constantly calling me critical.

A few days later, Cathy texted: "Good morning B, How are you?"

"Good morning Cathy, I feel pretty fucked up," I replied. "Still digesting my awful energy."

Then she answered: "I figured. But remember, it's not your awful energy. It's not even awful. It's just SAMSARA, the physics of perpetuation. *Acknowledge. Accept. Love.* That's our process, the way we break affliction cycles."

"I totally see the perpetuation in everything that had happened in my life. It's evident right now. I see the patterns and what triggered them. Everything clicked into its place. It's obvious what happened and why. Thank you for that!" I answered.

She responded: "Yes, that part is difficult to swallow. But again, we must think about our blind spots and places where our conduct still comes from shadowy aspects of the self, which are parts of the coping mechanism. So again, it's not you. I know this, so it's easy to love you no matter what."

Then I continued: "What bothers me is that you said that when you see my energy, you want to run away and not be close to it.

So, I'm unsure how to love and accept something that turns people off. I feel like I'm this nasty ball of energy that does repetitive things and makes people run away."

"Yes, but if you don't hear how judgmental energy or grasping or projection feel to others, you won't have grounds for transforming those inherited patterns. This is what I mean when I say that the whole awakening process depends on relationships."

Then she added: "Anyone who can really see you can see that you have a beautiful heart and a kind spirit."

If I had a beautiful heart and a kind spirit, then why did people hurt me? I thought.

PSYCHEDELICS

In search of more answers, I called the White Wolf, and we scheduled another treatment. Like before, he started by having me meditate on my intentions. Then, after an hour of this, I dove in. Again, I was lying on my couch, and again, he had me scan my body.

"How does it feel?" he asked.

"I feel severe pain in my right arm and shoulder," I said. "I feel like I can't move my hand and arm. It's like they don't belong to me."

Then he asked, "Can you sit up?" And so I did. "Now, ask your arm how it feels."

"It told me that it feels tired," I replied.

"Tired from what?" he inquired.

"From all of the holding it has been doing. Tired of protecting me."

He then asked, "How does the rest of your body feel about your arm?"

"It's angry," I said.

"Why is it angry?" he asked.

"Because the arm was stopping me from the things I wanted to do in my life."

"Now is the time to tell this part of your body that you love it," he said. "Simply thank it for serving you for all those years when you needed it. Thank it for protecting you."

So, I thanked my arm for protecting me all those years, and I told it that I loved it.

"But it's still excruciating," I said. "It still feels like it doesn't belong to me. Like prosthesis. It's been this way for such a long time that now the only thing it knows how to do is to defend."

"Is the rest of the body still angry with it?" he asked.

"No," I said.

"Just keep loving it. Keep reminding the rest of your body that it had its purpose, and be thankful for it."

It all seemed a little abstract, but it appeared very real. I could feel the anger radiating from the rest of my body. I felt the detachment of my arm and the sensation of severe pain as if it were an artificial limb that had been jammed into my shoulder.

Following the treatment, I felt like a different person. The sensation in my arm persisted, but now there was communication between us. Every time I felt it, I would catch myself having judgmental thoughts like, *"Why are you hurting me right now?"* Then, I would remember to be gentle to it, and I would send love and thankfulness towards it.

Most importantly, I now understood that whenever I really asked for help, and not just pity, I would always receive it.

BODY

The supervised psychedelic treatments, along with the additional therapy sessions, helped me to identify and release a lot of trauma. It felt like every life experience I had was somehow stored within parts of my body, just sitting there watching the show and attracting similar experiences. Gradually, all those emotionally overcrowded shelves I needed to clean up became lighter. It was like I could finally feel the real me coming out—the one I was meant to be before all the conditioning and negative experiences.

After working on releasing the emotions trapped in my body, I finally started to listen to what my body was saying. Through this process, I came to realize that I had never felt comfortable in my body. A big part of it was because my mother made sure I would not. In her eyes, there was always something wrong with the way I looked.

As far back as I can remember, she would drop suggestions that I was just a little bit overweight or sometimes I was too skinny. According to her, I was never in my perfect weight. Nor was she ever pleased with my body type. She used to say: "You have your father's body type. It's too bad you don't have my skinny long legs."

I must admit that, like most normal people over the age of twenty-five, my weight fluctuated by about twenty pounds. That fluctuation depended on my stress level and emotional state. When I was really stressed—during my immigration, my divorce, and my depression I wouldn't eat much, and I stayed skinny. When I was relaxed and at peace with myself, my weight was more on the average side. Even when I was transitioning from one state to another, I was never overweight or fat, not according to the weight standards anyway.

Not only was my body never good enough, but my hair and face also failed to live up to my mother's standards. My hair was either too long or too short, or I wasn't wearing it well enough to hide my round face—something she never missed an opportunity to bring up.

"Your cheeks are too big," she would say: "So you need to make sure you don't show them all. It's best to have a fringe and not put your hair in a ponytail. That way, the roundness won't seem so bad."

While going through all of those therapy interventions, I decided to be brave and try something I'd always wanted. I cut my hair in a short bob hairstyle and dyed it red. I loved how it turned out, and so did my friends. Even random people on the street, in the gym, and in stores paid me compliments.

A week later, I called my mother. I told her that I had cut and colored my hair.

"How could you destroy your beautiful, natural ash blond hair?" she said. "It's too early for you to start coloring it!"

"But I'm forty-three," I replied.

"It doesn't matter. You will regret it."

I could feel the blood rushing into my head, but I decided to breathe and say: "Well, it's my hair, and I can do whatever I want with it."

While still on the phone, I thought, *Why doesn't she even want to see a picture of it?* We could have connected through a video call. It would have been so easy for her to see me, but she wasn't interested.

Then, for the first time in my life, I felt sorry for her. *How was it possible not to approve of your child's appearance even once?* I thought. After all of my realizations, she no longer had the power to trigger me, but I still couldn't understand how it was that I was never good enough. Whether I was skinny or normal, whether in short or long hair; blond or red—according to her, I never looked good.

FORGIVENESS

I couldn't come to terms with the fact that what my parents did was acceptable. I think that a parent's responsibilities go beyond just creating life and meeting their children's physical needs. They must protect them from physical harm, not beat them. They must meet the children's need for love, attention, and affection, not abandon them. They must shield them emotionally, not make them suffer.

I tried to excuse my parents for their behavior and to forget what they did to me. It didn't work out. My memories wouldn't allow it. All of the stories remained, and they all demanded an explanation.

My therapist suggested that it would be helpful if I express my feelings in writing. She said that writing letters to everyone that hurt me would help me release the emotions that were stuck in me. I was skeptical about it, but I decided to try it.

I made a list of all of the people who had been hurtful to me. Next to their names, I wrote down what they had done to me. I wrote everything I could remember, down to the smallest detail. My memory of those hurtful moments was clear, and writing about it was painful.

The following week, I decided to write letters to both of my parents. Though I never actually mailed them, I used this exercise to express all of my anger, sadness, and disappointment. I started by writing that they shouldn't have made me in the first place if they didn't have the time and the energy to take care of me. I wrote about how deeply frustrated I was with them and with the way they treated me. Then, I forgave them for every single minor and major abuse and mistreatment I could remember. I forgave them for everything.

Afterward, I did the same with everyone else who had hurt me in some way. I spent days on every person, and I wrote down the most minute, most painful details I could remember.

And I forgave them all.

Last but not least, I had to forgive myself. That was the most difficult step. I wrote a letter to myself to forgive myself for all of the mistakes I have made. I forgave myself that I couldn't turn back time and change what had happened. I forgave myself for the fact that I rarely listened to or believed in myself and that I didn't respect or appreciate myself.

None of that forgiveness was easy. I struggled with them all. But by sticking to the process, I was able to let go of the pain I had held onto for so long.

BIRTH

During my fifth and last psychedelics session, the White Wolf asked: "Can you stand up and connect with the earth while at the same time connecting with the universe?"

I imagined myself as a tree with giant roots networked throughout the entire world and endless branches stretching out into the cosmos. The expanse felt endless.

After a while, he told me to come back to my body.

"How do you feel?" he asked.

I looked down, and what I saw surprised me.

"My legs look so lovely. My toes are so cute. And even my knees are beautiful."

With a big smile, I looked at him and continued, "I'm so happy to have them. It feels like they did a great job carrying me around all those years."

Then, I started to experience my arms and hands as if noticing them for the first time. With my right hand, I touched my left arm. I squeezed it up and down to make sure it was really mine. I did the same with the other side.

"They look so gorgeous," I said. "And my fingers are the perfect size for my hands."

I was like a little kid, full of curiosity, observing every little part of a discovery. I ran to the other room and looked at myself in the mirror.

There, I had the urge to take off all of my clothes so that I could see every little detail of my new body. But I didn't.

"Radiant," I shouted. "Look at my body. Wow! It's so gorgeous."

"Yes," he said. "You were always beautiful."

At last, I felt connected with my entire body. With each little cell. I was glowing.

It was the most extraordinary experience of my life. I almost heard the universe saying: *Welcome to the world, Borislava. You finally made it here. There is more work to be done, but now you won't be afraid of being you anymore.*

With a big smile on my face and enormous joy in my heart, I said, "This is me. At forty-four years old, I feel like I'm just being born."

But then, where had I been before? In a total disconnect... floating somewhere between the universe, the earth, and my body?

Finally, after four decades, I was happy to wake up in the mornings. I appreciated being in this body. I realized that it was a miracle to be on this Earth and be part of the universe.

MEXICO

After the forgiveness, the compulsion to write my story would no longer leave me alone. I followed my instincts and decided to give it a try. I researched extensively to find the perfect location for my work. I needed someplace warm, with scenic views, that was close to California.

Two months later, in January 2020, on the day after my birthday, I left for Cabo San Lucas. I took one small carry-on suitcase and a backpack. Inside were my clothes, a laptop, a little printer, and some paper and pencils. From the airport, I took a shuttle directly to the small apartment I had booked, and one hour later, I was settled in and ready to write.

Like many creative projects, mine grew well beyond its original vision. Along with the autobiographical vignettes, I decided to pair photography with each story to depict my experience visually. I also hired a welding artist to build a human-size birdcage. After completion, we assembled the cage in the living room of my apartment.

My work was well underway. Then, in March, the Mexican Federal and State Authorities declared a national health emergency.

The coronavirus was spreading around the world, and that changed everything.

One day, my mother, who rarely contacts me, decided to call.

"How are you," she asked. "Are you still in Mexico?" Then, with sarcasm, she added: "Are you going to become a Mexican now?"

"I'm just working on my book project," I told her. "I want to finish before I go back."

"Aren't you worried you might end up living in Mexico forever? If they close the borders, you will get stuck there."

"I have been living in fear most of my life," I said. "And I'm tired of it. Whatever happens will happen, but the fear will not control me anymore."

After hanging up the phone, I felt sad. She will never change, I thought.

All of my friends were trying to get me to come home, too. *What are you doing there?* they said. *Are you crazy?*

Soon, the restrictions began. First, they closed the yoga studio I was going to, then the restaurants. Later, the swimming pool shut down. The beach and the ocean were both forbidden. Without a car, I could only go to the small local grocery store, where one day, I couldn't even enter because I had no mask and nowhere to buy one. The bars of restriction were multiplying.

With all that pressure, I could feel my anxiety trying to sneak back in. It felt like I was going back into the cage—the cage I have been creating to protect myself ever since I was born. This time, it surrounded me on all levels, both emotional and physical. Not only was my anxiety standing manifest in my dark living room cave, where all of the windows had been covered with black paper for taking the pictures, but it was outside, too, in politics and society. The density of living with these many aspects was enormous. With each day, I felt like the walls were getting closer and the cage was getting tighter. There was almost no room for me anymore.

Nevertheless, I stuck with my plan and stayed in Mexico to finish my project. Because of the pandemic situation, the pictures were going to take longer, but I was no longer in a hurry.

FAREWELL

Finally, I finished writing the book and had my letter ready for potential publishers. After some resistance, I gathered my energy and sent my first email to one publisher. The following day, my sister called and told me that our mother had passed away.

The news crushed me.

Seven years before my mother had her first stroke. Luckily, this hadn't left her with any physical or mental consequences, thanks to her doctor friend.

During the pandemic, my mother became lonely and was unable to communicate with people because of the restrictions. Being socially active all of her life and not connecting with others put a lot of stress on her. That's when she had a second stroke.

My sister told me the hospital said it wasn't a big one and that our mother would recover quickly. Still, because it was during the pandemic, they released her after only four days instead of seven.

When she got back home, my sister moved in with her to help her with her recovery and the upcoming physiotherapy she was going to need. We were not talking very often after my so-called "awakening," but every once in a while, we would have a call. Our next call was not very long, but it was the last one I would have with her and one that I will never forget.

"How are you?" I asked.

"I don't feel good," she answered. "I don't want to burden you or your sister. I don't want to feel like I can't do things alone and that someone has to do them for me. I don't want to feel like a vegetable. I don't want to need help just to take a shower or go to the bathroom."

Then I said: "If you don't want that, then it won't happen. I wouldn't want that for any human being, and I certainly wouldn't want that for you."

Then, she changed the subject. "I want to tell you that family and close friends are the most important things in this life."

"I know," I answered.

"Nothing else matters," she said. "Also, I want to wish you lots of joy and all the best in your life."

And before hanging up the phone, she said, "I love you."

"I love you too," I replied, and we hung up.

The next day, my sister called to tell me our mother had another stroke—a massive one this time—and that she was in a coma. We knew that if she woke up, it would be tough for everyone. A few days later, she died.

After hearing the news, I cried for days. I was consumed by feelings of sorrow and guilt. I couldn't stop thinking about how, when I had sent that email to the potential publisher, she had decided to leave this world. It all felt like my fault.

SEPARATION

The guilt I carried about my mother's death was not something I could avoid. For some reason, I believed that the fact that I had sent my first email to that publisher had triggered something in the universe, causing her to pass away. *Was I not supposed to do that?* I thought. *Was the book writing just for me?* I didn't know. I was confused and in pain, and I decided to stop my attempt to publish and let it go until I felt ready to continue.

In the meantime, I reconnected with Cathy again. She came to visit Mitko and me in Cabo San Lucas. It was intense as always, but I wanted her to see my book, which I had printed a few copies of and proudly displayed on my living room coffee table.

Holding the book, she said nothing at all. Nothing like *you did a good job,* or *it looks nice,* or *can I read it,* or anything. Being a writer herself, I thought she would at least appreciate the hard work I put into it, but just like my parents, she remained silent until the end of her stay.

On her last evening with us, she hugged Mitko and me to say thank you and goodbye.

I finally asked her a question that had been haunting me since we met.

"Why are you putting one of your hands like a bird claw on my back behind my heart while you are hugging me? What is that for? Just your fingers are touching my back, but not your palm."

She looked at Mitko and me with surprise and said, "That's how I connect with people. The spine and vertebrae are the strongest part of the human body."

Then, visibly upset, she said, "Good night," and went to her bedroom.

In the morning, before I heard her exiting the front door, I had a dream. I was with her in a desert. Just she and I. Facing each other, I looked at my body and noticed it was covered with a spider net. I started taking it off and creating a big ball of it. When I was finally done, I reached out to her and said: "Here it is. This spider net is not mine, and you can take it back now." Speechless, she took it, and I woke up.

I haven't heard from her since.

About ten months later, I began to think that maybe the conventional publishing route was not for me. If I was going to continue with the attempt to make my book available to the public, I would need to do something different. I started researching the possibilities of turning it into an NFT (non-fungible token), a unique cryptographic asset used to create and authenticate ownership of digital assets.

With the ongoing research, I contacted friends who explained more. When I felt ready to step forward and make my first NFT, I got a call from my sister. At that time, a friend was visiting, and when I saw it was my sister calling, I said, "This is not good news. She almost never calls me."

It turned out that my instinct was right. She told me that our father had passed away. It was only one year and three days before that my mother had passed away. I was in such shock I couldn't even cry.

After hanging up, I asked my friend to stay and be with me for a few days. I didn't want to be alone and enter that dark space I knew might consume me.

While she was here, I told her that many of my dreams from the past few months had come true. Several times, I dreamed of him joining my mother. In those dreams, they were happy and dancing like I've never seen them do in real life.

Then it hit me again. *Why is this happening again right when I'm getting ready to publicize this book? What is going on here?*

Processing what had happened, I felt sad and disappointed that I'd never been able to connect with my father. I could never be the daughter he wanted, and he could never be the father I needed. *And now it is too late,* I thought. He is gone. None of that could be "fixed". There was no more time. At least I knew that I'd tried, and now the only thing I had to let go of was the failure of the attempt.

In confusion and pain, I again decided to stop the book release process and wait to see what the universe would unfold next.

RETREAT

Still searching for answers, I decided to participate in an Ayahuasca retreat. What better place to do so than Mexico?

I found a woman called Sage. She was originally from the United States but moved to Baja years ago and dedicated herself to facilitating psychedelic retreats, either alone or with other shamans. Sage was skinny, blond, and blue-eyed. She didn't have the shamanic look I had pictured in my mind—she looked like a model.

For this particular retreat, Sage was partnering with a native Mexican shaman called Tata. Before the actual retreat, there were a few video calls with Sage and the rest of the group. It turned out that the group would be tiny: three ladies from the United States and me. I loved the intimacy of the group and the fact that there was preparation with intention.

My intention was: *Should I try to publish the book, or should I leave it alone?*

After three weeks of working on our intentions, following a specific diet and exercise, the day of the retreat came. We all gathered in one place in San Jose Del Cabo, where a van with a driver was waiting for us.

After a half-hour drive, we reached the East Cape of Baja California Sur. There, we met our hosts and the second shaman, Tata.

He was as tall as me, skinny, with long black hair and immense eyes radiating happiness and love. He wore sneakers, jeans, and a T-shirt. When I saw him, I must have had a very surprised look on my face because one of the ladies said: "You should see him in his ritual clothes. He looks totally different then."

We were shown the grounds and the casitas where we were supposed to stay. For me, they chose a casita of about three square meters, with about a meter and a half of concrete walls, a wooden door, and a grass roof. There was a net around the top of the walls to allow for airflow and protect from insects. Inside was one twin-size bed and one chair. There was a single hook on the inside of the door where I could hang my towel. I thought it would have been nice to have a little table.

Before the ceremony, everyone went to their casitas to change and get ready. The ceremony was in a broad circular dirt area without grass or vegetation. The shamans had already prepared their altars, the spots for everyone, and the firewood in the center. In honoring the four corners, each direction had a giant painting with an image of the animal representing that direction.

Because Ayahuasca is a female plant, the ceremony was supposed to start in the evening and continue throughout the night. Everyone was getting ready to settle into their designated place. There was a mat, a blanket, a different color candle in front of each of our spots, and a bucket with a lid for purging. As part of the preparation and to be more comfortable, I borrowed a light air mattress and a sleeping bag from a friend. I set up everything, including a small altar space where I kept my favorite crystals and other small objects.

Having lived in Mexico for a while, I understood that nothing here starts on time, and the ceremony was no exception. It took about two hours after the scheduled time for them to transform themselves into their shamanic clothing, prepare their altars with crystals, candles, feathers, copal, drums, singing balls, the brew with the medicine, and get the fire going. Tata explained about the ritual, the medicine, and the fact that we could always take more after the initial dose and also say no. It was our ceremony, and we could do whatever felt right. They were there to support us.

Then Sage and Tata started cleaning us with lots of copal and tobacco smoke. Tata administered a single dose of rapé, the name of a dried powdered tobacco snuff from the Amazon, where it is used as a powerful and beautiful healing medicine. That was something else I experienced for the first time. With a special little pipe made of bone, he blew deep into each nostril. It felt like someone cleaning the lining of the nostrils, passing through the left and right side of the brain, down the spine, and finishing at the tailbone. That medicine is used for grounding, centering of the self, and healing.

When that settled, Tata returned to administer some eye drops called Sananga that ultimately could help us with our visions, but it also has the ability to promote understanding and bring on a healing effect that is more spiritual than physical.

Then the time arrived. I was last in the circle, and I watched the ladies drinking the offered Ayahuasca tea brew. When my turn came, I felt a bit nervous, but I knew there must be a reason I was drawn here and that I shouldn't back off at the last minute.

AYAHUASCA

While Sage sang and drummed native American songs from which I only understood the words *Aya* and *Mother*, Tata offered me my first medicine cup. Before drinking it, I reminded myself of my intention and took it all. It tasted like a natural tea made out of plant roots. Then I waited.

I looked at the fire, submerged in the drumming and the songs, but nothing was happening. Some of the ladies started crying and making strange noises, but I remained fully aware of everyone and everything.

Tata noticed this and asked if I wanted to take a second cup of medicine. I said yes. I thought it must not have been strong enough. I don't know how much time had passed, but I still felt nothing while the others were already purging and making even louder noises.

Then, after some more time, Tata came to me and asked how I was feeling.

"I feel fine," I said.

"Do you feel the medicine?" he said.

"No," I replied.

At that point, I thought that I must be too blocked and controlling and that I was not allowing the medicine to penetrate my system.

"Would you like to smoke some Changa?" He asked.

"What is Changa?" I asked.

"It's like DMT," he said.

I felt that maybe, on top of everything, if I smoked Changa, it would be too much. But still, I found myself saying, *"Yes."*

Tata went to his altar and returned with a cigarette. He told me to smoke three times and to hold my breath for a few seconds while smoking. Even on the first inhalation of the substance, I could already feel it. With the second one, my awareness felt like it took a bullet train into the unknown. I don't think I even took a third puff. I remember that I couldn't sit anymore and had to lay down and move my spine like a snake. I was in.

What I experienced at first was metallic-sounding music. I was surrounded by many geometric shapes, but everything moved so fast that I couldn't understand it. Then I saw an image of something red and black. Hesitating to get close, I reminded myself there was nothing to fear. When I approached, I realized that it was the Earth. She was angry, sad and disappointed. She was crying on the outside and furious inside. Ready to erupt just like one giant volcano. I started wondering: *How much time do we have left?*

I left that scene and moved forward, arriving at something that reminded me of Las Vegas. There were swarms of colorful, geometric shapes, and within them, I saw cartoon-like people and buildings. I was walking on a pathway, and those entities were talking and reaching out to me on both sides. They were like us: different races with different occupations, calling me over, trying to sell something, wanting my attention. It was challenging to escape. Just like in Vegas, when you enter one casino, it catches you up like a vacuum, dragging you to another and another until, eventually, you are lost and can't go out.

I don't know how much time I spent trying to avoid getting sold by the *"Vegas People."* I knew they wanted to distract me and waste my precious time, so I made sure I got out of there as soon as possible.

Next, I saw myself as a book. A big, soft white book that almost felt like a pillow. Being that book, I heard voices telling me *You are the book. Don't you see? You are the book. Relax. Don't worry about it. It's in you. It's you. Relax now.* It felt good not to worry about it anymore.

ANCESTORS

Meanwhile, the person lying closest to me started acting strange. A loud voice that didn't sound like her own began to emerge from her. The voice was that of another woman, and I started to worry. It was as if an entity were possessing her, and it reminded me of my Santa Cruz experience. When I opened my eyes, I couldn't believe what I saw.

She moved like a serpent, making sexy noises while the trees behind her swayed and whispered along. In the distance, dogs were barking, and nearer, I could hear cows from the neighbor's ranch being restless. In one of the nearby trees, I heard an owl hiss. The energy seemed dark and heavy, and I got scared.

Part of me wanted to go back to my journey and enjoy my time with those unearthly colors, shapes, and worlds, but the other part of me was freaking out. My mind kept saying: *What if that entity decides to change the vessel and gets out of her and comes into me? I can't go back and experience that nightmare again.*

Split into two parts, I didn't know what to do, but the desire to be safe prevailed. I gathered my energy and forced myself to sit up. I looked around, trying not to close my eyes and fall back into my journey. It was like I was in a scary movie. Dark shadows were creeping around the trees and whispering; the birds and animals in the background were making noises. It felt like a dark energy cloud was all around us. Looking closer, I saw Sage holding a stick of wood and tracking a circle around us in the dirt. *She's protecting us,* I thought. *So it's not my imagination or the medicine. All of those things that I hear and see are there. Now what?* It feels like it's going to be a long night.

After a little while, I threw up and felt better, but the woman's possession voice was getting louder and wasn't stopping. I wanted to get back to my journey, but I couldn't allow myself to do so. I need to be present and in my body right now. Then I remembered the cards I withdrew before the ceremony. They were *Ancestors, Owl, Wisdom,* and *Bones* for casting deviation. In an instant, I knew what I had to do.

From the little altar before me, I picked up my round obsidian crystal. With my other hand, I picked up the blue evil-eye key I'd purchased in Turkey years ago. Then, I called on all my ancestors and imagined them above me. My mother's lineage was on my left side, and my father's was on my right. I felt their energy and support. I knew they were protecting me.

Desperate to stay as present with my body as possible, I started tapping the obsidian ball against the inside of my wrist bones. It felt better. I felt alive. Altering the tapping hands, I continued to do so for a while, but the medicine was kicking in, and I had a tough time staying with my body. I struggled to convince myself that the protective songs, drumming, fire, and candles protected me and that I was safe, but in the back of my mind, I couldn't stop thinking: *What if that entity comes to me? What will I do then?*

In desperation to stay with my bones and body, I called in my mother. She arrived immediately. I felt her energy and saw her silhouette. Afraid she would judge me for participating in a ceremony like this, I asked for her help. She agreed and said all I had to do if I needed any help with anything was to ask her in my mind, and she would be there for me. Without any feeling of judgment or criticism, she placed herself between me and that entity to protect me like a shield.

For a moment, I sat with tears in my eyes, overwhelmed by the immense unconditional love I received from her and my other ancestors.

Then, in my mind, I asked my mom not to let me fall asleep. Finally feeling safe, I decided to lay down and look at the stars, where, to my surprise, I was able to see all of the constellations present. I wondered if the people who saw and drew them ages ago were using Ayahuasca or some other plant medicine to be able to see them and draw maps of them.

Tired and lost in the sky, I must have fallen asleep. The next thing I remember is leaping up from my mat. Right behind me, a screaming cat sprinted toward our circle. I realized that my mom must have called on that cat to wake me up.

Waiting for dawn, I sat and stared at the fire, thankful to my mother and ancestors for their help. Before that, I had never been grateful to them for giving me life and supporting me in my journey.

PURPOSE

Following the ceremony, the answers to my intention questions became clear. I knew deep down in my gut that everything I had experienced in my life had its purpose. Nothing was random, and it was something I had agreed to go through before I reincarnated into this life. The wide variety of experiences gave me a broad view that connected me with many people on a profound level of understanding.

After a few months of reflection, it became clear to me that I wanted to help others. Inspired by the teachings of Dolores Cannon, I pursued what I thought was the most comprehensive training in regression therapy. I became a certified quantum healing hypnosis therapist and to complement my skills, I trained in clinical hypnosis.

The sessions use powerful hypnosis techniques for accessing that all-knowing part of ourselves called the Higher Self, which resides beyond the conscious mind. Sometimes, mental and physical ailments are rooted in trauma from past lives; sometimes, they are connected to a person's present life. Whatever the case, the Higher Self reveals the cause and will assist according to any soul's lessons. My job is to guide, hold space, and assist.

The sessions are designed to be long, sometimes up to eight hours. They are divided into parts: in the first, the person talks about their life; in the second, I hypnotize them and regress them to a past life or some other existence they may have had; and in the third, I connect them with their Higher Self, where they can ask questions that they have prepared in advance about themselves and their lives.

After completing and graduating, I started practicing.

One day, a woman came to me. After the initial conversation, during which she told me about her life, what was going on with her, and her focus and intention for the session, we moved to the second part. There, I invited her to lie on the bed, asked her if she felt comfortable with the temperature, and told her I would guide her into a light trance-like state by helping her focus on her energy, breathing, and visualization.

Everything was going smoothly, and with my guidance, her Higher Self showed her a past life in which she was a woman who lived in the Middle East, was from a high-class family, and had to be negotiated/sold to someone so that peace in the area could be kept. After she learned the lesson and the purpose of that life, I guided her to a second one.

There, something strange happened. In her second life, she married a person in a sacred ceremony surrounded by people in a circle. Everyone was wearing black, including her and her husband-to-be. During that sacred wedding ceremony, they performed a blood oath ritual where they made a small cut on their fingers and swore an oath. She promised him that her soul would always be together forever with his.

When I asked her to look into his eyes and tell me if she knew the person from that previous life in her current one, she said, "Yes."

It was her ex-husband, to whom she was feeling very attached. He had been making her sick to the point where she couldn't move forward with her life even though they were divorced.

Then she suddenly began crying and screaming and shaking on the bed, convulsing with a changed voice. It was similar to the woman from the Ayahuasca ceremony and in my mind, I thought *The Universe is testing you again, Borislava. Now, what are you going to do? You can't run and leave her there. This time, it is your responsibility to help.*

Crying and screaming, she was saying: "I'm possessed by the devil. I see the most dark energy I could imagine in the universe."

Shaking and sobbing, she continued, "He had a million lives and was made out of the bones of the dead. Bones of people he made suffer. He is a dead man walking. He gets his life force from the devil."

Calmly and without fear, I asked her: "Did you choose him to make you stronger?"

"Yes!" She said.

I continued, "Do you want me to help you break that oath and have no more energetic attachments to him?"

"Please do," she answered.

Then I guided her to go back to that time and release her oath with love and understanding for both of them. Understanding that it had its purpose for that lifetime, but it doesn't serve a purpose in this lifetime, I guided her to release the energy she was seeing and feeling all around her. Sobbing and making rapid gestures with her hands, she slowly started to let that energy leave her and started to look and feel a bit better and calmer.

In the end, she said, "I'm clean now."

Before I counted her up, I wanted to make sure that there was no lingering residue of possession, and I asked her Higher Self to scan her body to make sure no leftover energy from the ex-husband or any other entities remained. The answer came back that she was clear now, and she would feel much better in the weeks to come.

During integration, we sat to talk about what had happened. She was surprised, thankful, and tired from the big shift in energy she had just experienced.

BLESSINGS

I had a dream.

I was in my hometown in Bulgaria, called Bankya. In front of the house where my mother grew up. There, on the big green lawn, I was sitting on a beach chair, holding my book in my lap. Next to me was someone I had never seen before. Looking into his eyes made me feel like he was my guardian angel. Delighted to be there together, we were looking at my book. Flipping page after page, I could feel his pride in me.

A few steps away, I saw my mother. She was wearing a dazzling white gown, and her hair looked longer, like in photos from when she was younger. My mother was dancing. I have never seen her express so much joy and happiness. The melody was in her mind, and I could feel the bliss radiating from her.

Then my father showed up, and they started dancing together.

While I was showing the book to my angel, I kept glancing over at my parents, watching for their reaction out of fear that they would be upset. But they didn't seem to care. All they wanted to do was dance.

Then I put the book on the tiny table in front of me. Both of my parents came and put their hands on top of the book. I saw how the energy and information from the book got out of it and went into their bodies and souls, like an electric exchange of information. In a split second, I saw them change by the information they had received. Happy and proud that I dared to do what I was supposed to, they hugged me and gave me their blessings.

When I woke up in the morning, I realized that neither my mother nor my father were angry at me. In fact, their souls were content, happy, and ready to go on their next soul voyage. Relieved by what I saw, I decided to move forward and publish this book.

I sincerely hope that everyone who reads it will find something that helps them along their path.

Pursue something you love, engage in it, and let it drive you.

THANKS

I want to thank Alex Todorov for his constant support—his belief in me and my journey made all the difference. Without his encouragement, BIRTHCAGE would not have been possible.

I am also grateful to Josh Wagner for his editorial work on the manuscript. His invaluable suggestions, comments, and corrections helped shape this book in ways I could not have done alone.

Special thanks to Emmanuel Novelo, for helping me with whatever I needed.

And to my friends and mentors, whose reassurance, guidance, and generosity made this journey possible. Thank you for standing by me and helping bring this book to life.

Thanks to you all.

Borislava

ABOUT THE AUTHOR

Born in Sofia, Bulgaria, during the era of communism, Borislava experienced a childhood shaped by restriction and adversity. Despite these challenges, she pursued education with determination, ultimately earning a master's degree in accounting and auditing.

At 25, she made a bold and life-altering decision to move to the United States in search of freedom and self-discovery. Immersing herself in creativity, she explored photography, graphic design, and storytelling—uncovering a newfound sense of purpose.

Her journey of transformation led her to study healing practices such as yoga, qi gong, shamanism, and secret plant medicine—deepening her understanding of consciousness and personal liberation. Drawn to the subconscious mind's power to heal, she now works with quantum healing hypnosis and regression techniques, helping others access deeper layers of self-awareness and healing.

Through BIRTHCAGE, Borislava empowers others to break free from the constraints of the past. Blending creativity, personal experience, and healing modalities, she guides individuals on a path of self-discovery, resilience, and transformation.

www.birthcage.com | www.borislava.com

ALSO BY BORISLAVA

BIRTHCAGE hardcover edition. The short stories in this book are visually unified through photographic representations of Borislava in a human-sized bird cage. Initially trapped, she gradually emerges, symbolizing a process of liberation.

ISBN 979-8-9914000-7-7

BIRTHCAGE ebook edition presents the collection of personal stories in their purest form, without accompanying photographs or statistics. This version focuses solely on the introspective narratives, offering a deeper connection to the transformative journey.

ISBN 979-8-9914000-1-5

The Spanish editions of BIRTHCAGE are titeled LA JAULA.